DESIRES' GUARDIAN

TEMPESTE O'RILEY

Dreamspinner Press

Published by
Dreamspinner Press
5032 Capital Circle SW
Suite 2, PMB# 279
Tallahassee, FL 32305-7886
USA
http://www.dreamspinnerpress.com/

Desires' Guardian
© 2014 Tempeste O'Riley.

Cover Art
© 2014 Reese Dante.
http://www.reesedante.com
Cover content is for illustrative purposes only and any person depicted on the cover is a model.

ISBN: 978-1-62798-999-2
Digital ISBN: 978-1-62798-927-5

Printed in the United States of America
First Edition
June 2014

This is for those who have come back from the edge, for those who still search for their heart, and for all who struggle with who they are.

Never give up!

acknowledgments

My eternal thanks to Nikki, Wolf, and Rowan Jade, for without each of you, Chase and Rhys would never have been.

chapter one

PLEASE, GOD, make it stop.

The loud ringing next to his head had Chase debating between smashing the phone and burying his head until the demonic thing went quiet on its own. When the ringing stopped but immediately started up again, he gave up on Option B.

Why?

Even mentally whining made his head hurt worse. Chase lay sprawled across his bed on top of the covers. The only part of him not exposed was his head; he'd burrowed under a pillow when the sunshine pushed its way into his bedroom. Sitting up without moving the pillow from over his head, Chase slowly scooped up his cell. "'Lo," he croaked.

"Chase?"

"Um, yeah. Who is—wait, James?" Chase's thoughts refused to clear as he fought his way past the alcohol struggling to drag him back into unconsciousness. The taste of stale beer and liquor was almost enough to make him puke. He vaguely wondered where his trash can was and whether he could get there if needed.

"You forgot, didn't you?" The loud chuckle that followed the question did not help with his headache. However, with everything that had happened recently—the stalking and threats against his best friend—he would have gladly suffered in silence to make James happy.

A soft moan escaped his dry lips. He tried to wet them with his tongue, but it felt dry and thick. "Sorry, Jamie. What did I forget?"

"You went out to the club again, didn't you?"

"Yes," he whimpered. "Dale and Simon wanted to go out for some fun. But I know you're not calling to see if I went home with anyone. So again I ask, *why* am I awake?"

"My art show tonight."

He was certain he could hear a smirk in James's voice. "It's"—Chase paused to check his clock—"not even noon yet, Jamie." He loved his best friend dearly, but why did he have to be so damned perky first thing in the morning?

"Lunch. Remember?"

Lunch? Eating? He *so* didn't want to think about food right then.

"Right. Let me get up and get dressed. I'll swing by your place soon."

"Go ahead and meet me at the restaurant, please. We have reservations at Zarletti's downtown. I'm out and about right now. Okay?"

"Uh, sure, hun." After a few more pleasantries, he hung up and slowly dragged his groggy self out of bed, stopping to down a couple of Tylenol and a full bottle of water before taking his shower.

Chase took his time getting dressed, and not simply because his head still hurt, the dull ache grating but livable. He never went out without dressing for the occasion, though it was nothing compared to how he would look later that night when he accompanied his best friend to his first gallery show. It would be James's debut as the featured artist.

God, means I'll have to deal with Rhys too. He knew Rhys wouldn't miss the show. He rolled his eyes for thinking about the damn man. Rhys was sex on legs, but his attitude was crap! Still, dressing to kill might not be a bad idea....

Chase finished buttoning the deep green silk shirt over his slight frame as he walked to the fridge in his small but well-appointed kitchen. Grabbing a bottle of Mountain Dew, he took a gulp before he put the cap back on, grabbed his backpack, and headed out the front door. He was usually a cappuccino kind of guy, but sometimes one needed an extra kick of sugar and caffeine, fast.

Yawning, Chase got into his car and started over to James's before he remembered they were meeting at the restaurant instead. At some point, he knew he would have to change his thinking and acknowledge that the little cottage was James and Seth's now, especially since they were not only living together but would be married in just over a month.

Chase turned the corner to pull up in front of Zarletti's. A moment later, a motorcycle passed him. He paused a moment to take in the eye candy: the black and chrome Harley Softail *and* the tall, wide-shouldered man atop it. When he parked, he realized to whom the bike belonged and groaned, cursing his luck and his reaction.

There Rhys stood, peering at him from beside the motorcycle. *Too bad the bike and those looks belong to such an ass hat.* Since the man was staring at him so blatantly, Chase decided to return the favor. He took a moment to let his gaze wander from the man's deep auburn hair and perpetual five o'clock shadow to his delicious athletic build, wide shoulders, and the defined pecs his black T-shirt served to accentuate, not hide, even with the leather coat half covering him. Rhys was huge at close to six and a half feet. He continued his perusal down Rhys to his thick, muscled legs and his chunky black leather boots. Chase allowed himself a soft sigh. He took just as long on the return trip, making a true production of it. When his gaze finally landed on Rhys's deep green eyes again, he smirked, turned, and made sure to put a little extra swish into his hips as he sauntered up the sidewalk to the front doors.

He reached to open one but paused when he heard the crunching of boots on the path behind him. He groaned to himself quietly and then stepped inside, hoping Rhys was there to meet someone else, not James. *Please let it not be us!* Chase had managed to avoid Rhys for the last few months, ever since James's first gallery show. It was a lot harder to stay away from him than he had expected. He hated how Rhys had befriended James, making avoiding him all the more complicated.

"Good afternoon, welcome to Zarletti's. Table for two?" the bright-eyed hostess asked as Chase approached her stand.

"No. I'm meeting someone. James Bryant? He should be here already."

"Very good, sir. And you?" the hostess asked, gazing past Chase to Rhys.

"The same, thank you." Rhys's deep, rumbling voice sent a jolt through his system, as always.

Chase tensed when he heard Rhys's reply. His smile fell, but he refused to look at Rhys again.

She promptly led them to a small corner table where James sat, his forearm crutches leaning against the wall behind him.

"Glad you could make it, Rhys," James called over Chase's shoulder. "Nice timing, Chase. You look better than you sounded on the phone."

"I'm okay, Jamie." Chase pushed away James's concern with a wave of his hand before he leaned in and kissed James's cheek. "How did you get reservations so fast?"

"I've had the reservations, Chase. Why do you think I called to make sure you were awake?"

Chase noticed the way James's eyes lit up when he saw him and how huge his smile was, which made him happy he had gotten up. However, what little enthusiasm he'd had for lunch died as soon as he realized Rhys was going to join them. He couldn't help it. Every time he looked at the man, he reacted, but after the way Rhys had treated him the night they met, and a few times since, he wanted nothing to do with the ego or the jerk. Straight people not understanding him was one thing, but a gay man making snarky comments about him being less, or that being twink-like made him undesirable? Beyond not cool! *Sadly,* Chase thought as he peeked at Rhys again, *I'd still take him home if he'd let me. See who is pinned against the floor screaming then!*

"I guess I didn't remember you telling me where we were eating," Chase explained as he sat beside James. "Don't mind me, hun. Now, why has our BFF date been hijacked and why is *he* here?"

"Come on, Chase, I'm hungry. No pouting."

He closed his eyes and took a few deep breaths to clear his irritation and worry. "My apologies. How about... what's on the agenda, my dear?" He folded his hands to make a small stand and rested his chin there, batting his eyelashes at James for full effect.

"Better," James said with a low chuckle. "I suppose we can tend to business first, though that won't get you out of here any faster." The stare accompanying James's words had him pinned to his seat. He sat up straight, suddenly wondering exactly why James had invited Rhys along.

What business could there be between the three of us?

4

"Business first is fine, James," Rhys rumbled. "Though I'm still not sure how you think Mr. Manning can help."

"What are you two needing help with?" Chase's eyes flitted between his best friend and the man he simultaneously wanted to throttle and devour. He cursed his dick as it stood up and took notice of Rhys's closeness.

"Not us, Chase. Rhys needs the services of a tech god. One that is good, discreet, and," James paused and shared a look with Rhys, "creative? But he doesn't believe you would agree to work for him, even temporarily."

"Tech god? Really?" Chase giggled before the rest of what James said sank in. "Wait, you want me to help Rhys with some computer problem? Why not just call the Geek Squad and have them fix it?"

"Chase."

"Why me?"

"I told you he wouldn't agree, James. I need a hacker or cracker or what-the-hell-ever they want to be called, not some wannabe desk jockey who thinks he's too good for anyone," Rhys grumbled. The look of disgust irritated Chase more than the words, though they didn't go unnoticed either.

"If anyone thinks he's too good, it's you, you pom—"

"Chase!"

"Fine," he snapped. He waved one long, slender hand toward Rhys as he continued. "What possible help could I be to *him*?" He couldn't bring himself to willingly address Rhys directly—snapping at Rhys didn't count. "Desk jockey?" "Wannabe?" The insufferable man might be nearly a foot taller than him, but he itched to teach him some manners.

"Chill for a minute, please. Rhys, as you know, is a PI and a bodyguard." When Chase nodded, James continued. "He's doing some work, though I don't know the details, and needs someone with serious computer skills but can't use his usual person. I was hoping you would help him."

James, the traitor, motioned Rhys to speak.

"Mr. Manning, James said you left Skye Designs and do consulting and freelance work now. He and Seth claim you're the best, so I am here

5

to hire you. If you agree, you will be paid for any and all work. I'm not asking a favor, I'm offering you a business proposition."

Chase listened as Rhys spoke and watched as emotions played across his face. Irritation, curiosity, worry…. Chase pursed his lips, glancing between James and Rhys. *Work with Rhys? Is James nuts?* He dropped his gaze to his wine glass and shook his head as he thought about working with Rhys Sayer—egomaniac, ass hat, sex god. If it was for Mark Gentry, Rhys's business partner, he would say yes right way, but could he deal with Rhys that much?

Rhys crossed his powerful arms. "I should go, Jay. I don't want to mess with your buddy-date thing or stress you before your show tonight. I retract my request, Mr. Manning." He raised one huge hand, motioning their server over. "Can you box mine, please?"

James sighed and frowned, a look Chase hated to see.

"Wait," Chase countered. "Do you really need IT help with your company? And why can't your normal guy work it? Surely you have one on staff."

James's lips twitched, and Chase knew he'd been had, but then, he never said no to James anyway, so why start now?

"Pouting won't help, Chase. Be good."

Chase rolled his eyes but couldn't help smiling. "Brat."

"My normal *guy* would be pissed at being called a guy," Rhys explained and smirked. "Kailee just got married and moved, with her new husband, across the country. She could still do part of what I need, but I would rather have someone local, especially for this sort of work. She agrees with James about your tech skills, so I'm willing to try you." Rhys flushed red, his eyes going round and wide. "I mean…. Oh, never mind. Will you help or not?" he grumbled.

DANNI BURNS, James's seven-year-old stepdaughter, and Rhys sat on a blanket in a glade dotted with small flowers near a gently winding brook, having tea, Rhys in his biker leather and Danni in one of her lavender princess dresses. Mrs. Rainbow—her beloved pastel, tie-dyed bunny in a tiny white-and-green Irish dancing dress with miniature black Mary Janes—rested between the two.

"So what do you think?" James asked, startling Chase out of his musing as he stood before what was secretly one of his favorite paintings of the collection. The gallery show had opened about an hour earlier, but the two men hadn't had much time together to discuss what images would be shown. Honestly, the fact there was such a family feel to part of the images, as opposed to James's usual erotic content, surprised Chase.

"I think you caught the mischief and sweetness of Danni beautifully." In truth, he was in awe of how James managed to capture both of their inner selves so perfectly. In his opinion, it was one of James's best paintings. The gentle giant and his precious little sprite. "But why did you pair her with Rhys of all people? He's so…." Chase trailed off, caught again by the striking masculinity before him.

"Powerful? Handsome? Gentle?" James raised an eyebrow at Chase and smiled. "I honestly wish you would tell me why all the animosity between you two," he added, voice soft.

"It doesn't matter, Jamie." He wrapped one arm around James's shoulders. "Come on, show me around some. I hear the artist is supposed to be pretty good, after all," Chase teased.

"Oh, you think he might be better than me?"

Chase would do anything to keep the huge grin gracing his best friend's face right then. "Maybe," he singsonged. Considering him for a moment, Chase took James's hand. "Seriously, you've outdone yourself. I'm so proud of you."

James blinked and looked up, smiling, his cheeks pink. "Thank you, Chase."

"James, it's time." Seth's voice broke their moment, startling both men. "Gather up your Chase and hurry, please."

Chase looked over to Seth, confused about what he was referring to. *The show isn't over, so where is he taking Jamie, and what does that have to do with me?*

"Oh! Oh, good. Come on, dear." James pushed him toward Seth and then maneuvered on his forearm crutches to follow behind.

Chase followed obediently, confused but moving with the flow of bodies around him. "What's going on, guys?" he asked once they were at the front of the gallery. He looked around and noticed there was a large covered frame that hadn't been there earlier.

7

Rhys's brother, Dal, sidled up beside Chase, bending to whisper into his ear, "He's got one last painting to reveal, but it's a special one. I heard not even Britt"—the owner of the gallery—"has seen this one."

"Really?" He peered up at Dal, again noticing how much he looked like Rhys, only a couple of inches shorter and a few pounds lighter.

"Shh… he's getting ready to speak."

Chase realized James now stood in front of the painting, smiling again.

"First, let me thank everyone for your warm reception and the wonderful turnout. As some of you know, I don't really do speeches, but this last painting is special. I debated showing *Inner Light,* but in the end decided others needed to see the subject as I do." James moved to the side, releasing his grip on one forearm crutch. He touched the sheet but didn't move it yet. "You see, sometimes when people reveal who they truly are inside, we find a vile, rotting corpse, but other times, what we find…." He trailed off and touched a recessed panel.

The sheet, which Chase realized was actually a curtain, slid aside to reveal a painting of… him! Well, it was him, but not him at the same time. The artistry was magnificent, but over half his face a lion was superimposed. The lion part even had his ear cuff clipped to the furry ear. Chase gaped, barely noting the gasps and clapping that burst all around him.

Chase moved to the side, trying not to attract attention as questions and praise swarmed James. He couldn't stop staring at the painting, trying to see how it could possibly be a representation of himself, but couldn't. He wasn't powerful or strong like a lion. And while he knew he was decent looking, the man in the painting had an ethereal beauty that dumbfounded him. It was both humbling and uncomfortable to look upon and hear Jamie's voice in his head saying that was how he saw him.

Chase was startled out of his thoughts when two of his friends, Simon Tyler and Dale Miller, nudged him. "Chase! Did you know about the painting? It's amazing," Simon gushed.

Chase shook his head. "I didn't. He can't really see me that way, can he?"

"With as much as you've done over the years to help and protect him, yeah, I think that's exactly how he sees you," Dale replied. "Of course, he's obviously blind. But then, if he showed you as you really are, no one would buy his artwork." Dale and Simon cackled, and Chase glowered at the both of them.

"Maybe he's trying to make up for conning you into working with Rhys," Simon suggested.

"Harrumph! I still can't believe I said yes, but you really think all this was planned? Seriously?"

"Eh, ignore Simon."

"We're going out tomorrow night to forget about the sexy ox, so don't sweat it," Simon said and winked. "Now, go congratulate James and smile. You look totally wrong with the scowl on your pretty face," he instructed, turning Chase and pushing him toward the now advancing James.

chapter two

DALE MILLER shook Chase awake when he pulled up to the curb in front of Chase's apartment building. Chase realized, belatedly, that he probably should have stayed in the night before. The sleep deprivation was not going to make spending the next nine hours or so at work, dealing with Rhys, any easier. He'd regretted agreeing to the date the previous night about ten minutes after John, his blind date, arrived. He'd told Simon setting him up was a bad idea, but those big, brown puppy eyes always got him into trouble—*every damn time!* Of course, he regretted agreeing to work for Rhys Sayer too, but his ability to tell James "no" was worse.

"Come on, buddy. You have work to get to. So do I." Dale didn't look much more awake than Chase felt, but he dutifully nodded and managed to remember to unbuckle before he got out of Dale's little green Toyota Yaris.

"Thanks," Chase mumbled as he grabbed his jacket and shuffled off toward his apartment on the second floor.

He stopped in his kitchen long enough to start the coffeemaker before heading to his room to strip. Chase glanced at his alarm clock and winced at the time. It was a little after six, Monday morning. Once his clothes were off and in the hamper, he padded into the bathroom to take a hot shower. He firmly believed sweat and smoke on a body were *not* attractive the next day. He cleaned up and got dressed, only fumbling with his slacks twice. He took one last look in the mirror and grimaced at the somewhat haggard look in his eyes. *Bad date followed by friend crying over a broken heart.... Never again, please!*

Chase made sure to put his leather cuff back on his left wrist, covering the scar there, and willfully ignoring the memories that always threatened to resurface when he was too tired. It and the silver spoon on a choker, he never left home without. He idly toyed with the double buckle as he thought about what John had said the night before, but wearing a leather cuff did not make him a sub or a bottom, no matter what anyone else thought.

Chase was thankful for the light traffic on his way to The Coiled Dragon Agency, the PI and bodyguard company Rhys and Mark owned. His mind wandered as he drove, reflecting on the changes in his life since he'd left Skye Designs. He'd only stayed so long in the first place to be there for James, but now that James only worked for them on a consulting basis and had dedicated himself to his art career, there was nothing to keep Chase there anymore. Starting his own consulting firm had terrified him at first, but he loved the freedom. Besides, it allowed him to still act as James's assistant when needed.

He made it to the site right on time. He hoped his annoyance and exhaustion wouldn't be too visible.

Shoving his keys into his pocket, Chase stepped out of his light blue Cruze, tilted his head back, and welcomed the crisp cool air and bright morning sun as it beat down on him. He knew he needed to wake up more and stop scowling before he met with Rhys, but his nerves had been on edge ever since he'd said yes two days ago.

He took a deep breath, then turned and headed toward the office. Chase's phone rang as he reached for the door. "Manning," he answered, no longer hiding the lilt he normally spoke with. He was his own boss now, and he refused to tone down or hide who he was ever again.

"Chase Manning?"

"Yes, this is Chase."

"Good. I have the right number." He recognized the voice but couldn't put his finger on who it was, not with the loud, rumbling background noise.

"Yes, you have my number. Now, do I get to know who you are, or should I hang up?" he teased.

It kind of sounded like Dal, but the chuckle that came through the phone went straight to his gut. "I had you pegged for the studious type that always checks the screen before answering." He knew that voice now: Rhys.

"What can I do for you, Sayer?"

"You can stop right where you are and not go in that door."

Chase's head popped up. He looked around the driveway and the street quickly, not amused when he noticed nothing around him but normal morning traffic. The office was in a converted house; the first floor was the agency. He knew the two floors above were living quarters, though he didn't know who lived up there.

"Why?" he ground out. "I'm here as a favor to you because James wants us to work together. For now." He needed more caffeine and sleep if the man was getting to him this fast.

"Mark was called away on another job. I'm on my way back now, so if you go in, you'll be breaking in, as no one's in the office."

Chase ground his teeth as he counted to ten in his head.

"You could have— Whatever, just hurry up or I'm going back home. Even empty, my bed is more enjoyable than you." Chase snapped his cell shut and slipped it back into his pocket, but immediately drew it back out again and sent a short text to James.

»I SO hate you right now! XOXO«

Right after he hit send, he heard the unmistakable sound of Rhys's Softail.

His cell chimed.

»LOL« was all James replied.

Chase had debated riding his metallic blue Sabre to work, but between his exhaustion and the fact Rhys would probably think he was "trying too hard" or something equally asinine, he'd driven his car.

Rhys rode up and parked his bike next to his Cruze. Watching the mountain of a man move to stand and dismount the bike had his mind wandering everywhere it shouldn't and his gaze glued to the hard, tight jeans-clad ass before him. Chase spun around fast to face the door when Rhys started to turn, not about to let The Ego know how much he was lusted after.

RHYS TOOK his time parking and dismounting his motorcycle. He hoped to maintain his aloof demeanor, though God knew it was hard to do with

Chase standing there waiting on him. Chase was dressed in a light blue button-down shirt with fine dusky blue vertical stripes that conformed to his lean and lithe chest and abs. On his slender hips hung a pair of low-rise black jeans that were faded on the thighs, ones he was certain Chase knew showed off his form well. His black leather belt had a twin, double buckle that matched the leather wrist cuff he always wore.

Rhys's gaze flicked up to Chase's face, and he looked into his eyes, mesmerized by the swirling colors framed by thick chestnut lashes. Chase's eyes were one part blue and three parts green, with the most beautiful flecks of gold in them that seemed to follow the path of where one color merged into the other. He had never seen eyes with two distinct colors like Chase's, much less with the intricate, almost lace-like patterns throughout the iris. Then he fixed on the silver hoop through the full, pouty bottom lip on the most beautiful, delicate, yet masculine face he had ever seen.

He broke from gazing at Chase with a slow blink, trying desperately to regain his self-control and professionalism. Keeping a firm grip on his helmet, Rhys strolled to the office door, unlocking and holding it open for Chase to enter ahead of him. He quickly disarmed the alarm and turned on the lights.

"Nichelle, our receptionist-slash-office manager, will be here in a few minutes. Until then, let me show you around and introduce you to your new office area. It's set up how Kailee wanted, but you're free to modify it however you desire. Computers aren't my thing really, but Kailee swore this was the best for what we needed."

"I checked out this Kailee of yours yesterday, and while I brought some of my own equipment, she's got a killer rep. So if she designed it, I'm sure it will suffice."

Chase restrained his words and voice a little more than he expected. Rhys couldn't help but be enchanted at the wide eyes roaming over the equipment or at Chase bouncing in place as he started touching different items.

"Come on. Let me show you where things are before you go all geek on me," Rhys said with a rumbling laugh.

Chase froze, hand outstretched. He turned his head toward Rhys, licked his lips, and then asked, "*Go geek*? Really?"

Rhys swallowed hard at the flare of heat in Chase's eyes but quickly shook it off. "Is it nerd, not geek?"

Chase growled, his lips compressed as he squinted up at Rhys. "Why don't you go lift something, or whatever it is you lumbering brutes do, and I'll go back to my car," Chase snapped.

"I wasn't trying to insult you, Cha—" Rhys stopped midword at the look on Chase's face. "I mean, Mr. Manning. You just seemed so... I don't know, giddy. I didn't want to get in the way once you started working on the system. But, um, Nichelle has all the codes and things you'll need, so...."

Chase looked past Rhys, stomped back out to the main area, and slowly turned in place. After a few moments, he stopped, faced Rhys again, and started talking. "Reception," he said, pointing to the large, curved wood desk near the front. "Waiting area, obvious by the chairs, couches, table, and reading materials," he continued, again gesturing with his slender hands. "Tech is here, of course," he added with a mischievous little smirk that made Rhys want to lick it off his face. "And I would hazard a guess that the two doors over there lead to Mark's and your offices, yours being the one closest to the front door. Kitchen, restrooms, and of course, storage. Did I miss anything?" Chase added with a grin.

Rhys sighed, shaking his head. "No, not really. You're good on details. Impressive. I'll just get out of your way, then, so you can get everything set how you want."

"Might be nice to know what I'm setting up to do, Rhys."

"You'll be doing net research some," Rhys explained. "We'll also need you to do some digging through computers, phones, et cetera. It just depends on the case at the time." He rubbed his eyes before continuing. "And yes, that means hacking into things here and via the net occasionally. I didn't mess with how Kailee left things, but I figured it's like anything else—you'll want things where you want them and not where someone else would."

Rhys turned to go to his office when Chase nodded his agreement, but drew up short when he heard the bell chime, letting him know someone was entering the office.

He moved around to the front and spotted Nichelle coming in, weighed down with goodies. "Lord, woman, what all did you get? It's just the three of us for now."

"Oh shush, you. You said the boy loved mocha but didn't bother to find out what kind, so I called Mr. Bryant and asked him. So I have a peppermint-and-white-chocolate mocha for him, a regular coffee for you, my drink, and a chocolate cheesecake brownie for you each. Now, where's our new computer boy?"

Rhys laughed at her rambling. He had adored her since the first time they met, back when she was dating his little brother, Dal. However, he was happier with her working for him than her dating Dal. "You two will get along great. Chase is already in the tech cave."

"Actually, I'm right here." Rhys turned and found Chase walking up behind him. Chase extended his right hand to take Nichelle's, bending to kiss the back of it before placing his other hand lightly on top. "Charmed. You must be the infamous Nichelle I've heard so much about."

She giggled, blushing slightly. "And you, sir, are quite the little charmer, aren't you? James and Dal warned me about you."

Chase flashed her a bright smile, which drew more giggles. "My dear, I am many things. A few of them are even safe for public consumption. Now, did I hear something about a mocha, 'cuz I know I smell one," Chase purred, sniffing the air lightly.

Oh God! Rhys grabbed his coffee and brownie and quickly fled to his office, closing the door before letting out the breath he'd been holding. *I am never going to survive having him work for me. Why did I listen to Seth and James?*

"Why does he have to be so beautiful?" Rhys mumbled as he sat down at his desk, wanting to find his work for the day distracting, though he didn't hold much hope.

LEANING BACK in his office chair, eyes closed, Rhys struggled with his mixed desire and fear. He had long ago given up on doing the books. On his best day, numbers barely held his attention, but today Rhys's chest ached from the expression of hurt and frustration on Chase's face that kept drifting into his imagination. He opened his eyes and drew in a deep breath, hoping to banish the phantom look. It didn't help any. The pains of his past and his fear of accidentally harming the young man again drowned out his appreciation of Chase's sheer beauty and sensuality.

Comparably, Chase was so fragile, so fluid in his movements and emotions. Rhys knew that were he to give in—if Chase would even consent to try a relationship with him—Rhys was certain he would come away more brokenhearted than he already was or be sent away for being too base a man. It had happened before, and he was determined not to go there again. Ever.

CHASE SPENT the next couple of hours continuing to set up and rearrange the tech area, impressed with everything already there. As Chase thought he had things the way he wanted them, he was snapped out of his musing by the loud clearing of someone's throat behind him.

"Um, Chase?"

He peered up from the floor where he was kneeling, having finished binding the cords up and out of the way completely, and noticed Mark Gentry standing in the entryway. "Oh, Mark, you scared me." He smiled to show he was teasing. "What do you need?"

The rumbling laugh Mark let out tickled Chase, who was glad he could interact with Mark without the drama and stress he had with Rhys. "Right. You, scared? You have to be the most non-scaredy cat person I know."

"Aw, you say the sweetest things," Chase cooed, batting his eyelashes and smiling.

"Yeah, yeah, yeah. Now, I need two things from you, if you can crawl out here for a bit." Mark stood over Chase, brow raised and a smirk on his lips.

Chase grinned wider and began to crawl forward.

"Like this?" he asked innocently.

"You're evil and you know it." Mark chuckled and took a step back, then motioned Chase to stand, which he did with his usual grace and fluidity.

"You are so not fun." Chase fake pouted. "Better now?"

"Yes, oh naughty one. Now, I need to see what you can dig up on this guy," Mark continued. He handed Chase a thin folder.

"Sure, but that's only one request. You said there were two." Chase sat at his desk and opened the file, checking what information Mark had provided. "What am I looking for exactly?"

"Financial issues mostly. He's the reason I wasn't here when you arrived. He's causing trouble for a client, and I have a suspicion on the why. I'm hopin' you can help me find the pieces I need to shut him down."

"That should be easy. I thought you guys needed help with something hard." Chase pouted, this time for real, as he still didn't see why Rhys needed *him* here.

"Ha-ha. I do, just not for this case."

"Oh, do tell."

The sudden flush that spread over Mark's face and down his neck surprised Chase. "I, um, it's nothing to do with work. It's a personal request?"

Chase smiled, motioning him to continue, curious what else his friend could need help with.

"I know it has nothing to do with work, but I hear you're good with cooking and wine and such, and I really need to impress my guests this weekend and kinda hoped you'd help me?" Mark explained, saying it all together as if it were one long word.

"Company? You're still seeing Aurora, right?" At Mark's nod, Chase continued. "So, whatcha need?"

"Her folks are coming to town." The miserable look Mark gave him had him fighting not to laugh. "And it's my first time doing the whole dinner-with-the-parents thing. Well, where I'm in charge, at least."

"All right, hun. Step one, breathe. Step two, let me get some work done and we can chat later about what all you need. Oh, and step three, relax. They are gonna totally love you! Now go, shoo, go on. Don't want my bosses getting upset with me for slacking off," he added with a wink.

Mark grinned as he turned away. Chase could hear him laughing all the way back to his office.

chapter three

RHYS WALKED beside Mark as they wandered the aisles at the Pick 'n Save, fighting the urge to laugh. Mark stood in the baking aisle, looking bewildered and clutching a typed list of ingredients. "Why do I need brown sugar, white sugar, *and* honey? And why does it matter if the salt is kosher or from the sea or not?"

"I don't know, man. It's your list," Rhys answered, failing to keep a straight face.

"But he swore I needed all this and that it would be easy to fix," Mark complained. "Should have let him do the shopping part like he suggested," he added under his breath.

"So why didn't you? And *who* is this mystery 'he'?" Rhys had been curious all week about whom Mark had roped into cooking for him. He knew Mark could cook but would be a basket case if he did so while trying to impress Aurora's parents.

"Huh? Oh, Chase is preparing our dinner tomorrow. Or rather, I asked him to help me cook and make sure things are nice and taste good together." Mark made his baking selections and continued to the next aisle, grumbling about why he needed three kinds of oil for one meal. Rhys stood there staring, lost in thought over visions of Chase in nothing but an apron. A short apron.

Mentally shaking off the inappropriate but delicious image, Rhys jogged to catch up. "Wait! Did you just say you conned Chase, as in Chase Manning, into cooking for your meet-the-parents dinner?"

"Yeah," Mark muttered as he consulted his list again. "Why? He made the menu and he's supposed to help, but he's not staying."

"God! You're trying to kill me."

Mark stopped to peer at Rhys. "I don't understand why it matters to you. He's doing this for me. You will have little to no contact with Chase, so whatever your issue is with him isn't a problem. Right?" he asked, his sudden scowl making Rhys step back at the implied threat.

"No, of course not," Rhys countered, shaking his head. "I'm just surprised, that's all."

The two large men continued through the store, garnering a few side glances, as they always did. After a few more aisles, Rhys cleared his throat. "Seth says Chase is really good at desserts, so that's good, right?"

"Yeah, I remember Seth talking about it when he was dating James, and James freaked out on him for a while." Mark smiled wide. "He said Chase coerced James into dinner with Seth at his place and that he helped with the cooking. If he's as good as James is, this dinner is going to make everyone happy. I just hope I can actually make whatever all this stuff is for. Even with help, I'm not sure about all this."

"YOU KNOW, when I asked for help I expected a *little* assistance, not you fixing such a fantastic smelling and looking meal. I mean, you even *made* the dessert!" Mark looked around his kitchen, wide-eyed.

Chase smiled at him. "You said you needed to impress Aurora's parents, so…."

"Yeah, that's true, but you did way above and beyond what I was expecting. I thought you would show me what to do and then leave me, not cook all this for me while you sent me out for flowers."

Chase shrugged and continued messing with the food.

"How'd you learn to do all this, anyway?"

"My mom loves to cook, and James was raised in a B&B. He learned to cook a lot of things and taught me after we met in college. It's no big, honest." Chase stopped to think through everything planned for the evening, not wanting to mess up Mark's big meet-the-parents thing. "Oh, Aurora said for you to set up the bar but not to worry about appetizers. So, from here forward, it should be super easy. I will stay in here, out of the way, and just serve. Once I deliver the main dish, I'll head out. All you'll need to do is serve dessert and then clean up. And, Mark?"

"Yeah?"

"Don't let Aurora clear the dishes if you want to impress her folks." Chase smiled, fussing with his cuff. "Show them you can take care of her, not that you expect to be taken care of."

Mark nodded as he again looked at the dishes and cookware in use. "I don't know how I'll repay you for this, but I swear I will, Chase!"

Chase waved away his words, unconcerned about "paybacks." They were friends: what else would he expect?

"Okay, so, what all are we having? I don't want to look like an idiot when her mom asks me about the food," Mark asked, scuffing the toe of one boot back and forth.

"Nothing too complicated. The winter fruit salad with lemon poppy seed dressing is already plated and in the fridge."

Mark's nose wrinkled. Chase broke off what he was saying and asked, "What?"

"It's not that weird, goopy marshmallow and fruit stuff, is it?"

Chase laughed at both the look Mark gave and his description. "No, Mark. It's a salad that has cranberries, apples, pears, romaine lettuce, and other normal salad ingredients in it, topped with the lemon poppy seed dressing I made this morning."

"So nothing weird or drippy or sticky?"

"Um, no." Chase fought not to laugh again, but it was hard with the earnest, worried look Mark was giving him.

"Now, your main dish is stuffed pork tenderloin with honey roasted baby carrots, and Parmesan-garlic mashed cauliflower. The crusty bread is cooling, and the butter is already out to soften. And for dessert, you have apple raisin crisp and vanilla bean ice cream."

"I'm going to have to practically live in the gym to burn off tonight's dinner," Mark teased, but Chase could see how pleased he was. Impressing parents was something Chase was good at; finding and keeping a decent man, not so much.

"Ha. Ha. Ha. Oh, I got both a red and a white for your dinner. Some people swear by one or the other, so they have a choice, but both pair nicely with the fruit and pork, don't worry."

The doorbell rang just as Mark's cell demanded his attention. Chase bounded off to answer the door for Mark, smiling widely at being able to cook for others who would appreciate it. Cooking was his one hobby. One that few knew about and fewer still would believe.

His grin froze when he opened the door and found Rhys standing before him with a rather expensive bottle of brandy in his left hand.

"Uh...." His mind went completely blank. Why was Rhys here? Now?

"Hi, Chase." Rhys extended his right hand. His smile was warm and open.

It took a moment, but his brain finally kicked in. Chase grasped Rhys's hand. He gasped at the spark of heat that flashed through him when their hands met. "H-hello. I didn't know you were coming to Mark's for dinner tonight."

Caught in Rhys's gaze, Chase couldn't seem to move away or say more.

Rhys's lips turned down. "He convinced you to cook for him but didn't tell you how many were coming for dinner? That doesn't sound like Mark."

Rhys released Chase's hand, the slow slide of heated skin against his leaving Chase aching and flushed. When he blinked, Chase was able to look away and take a steadying breath.

Mark interrupted the awkward moment when he came into the foyer and smiled at Rhys. "Hey, man, glad you made it before her parents arrived. Thanks. You got Ryan's preferred drink!"

"Of course. But, Mark, Chase says you didn't put me on the guest list."

"Yes, I did. I said three men and two women for dinner." Mark looked at Chase with his head tilted slightly. "Are you picking on Rhys again?"

"I—you—" Chase huffed. "I don't pick on Rhys," he snapped, folding his arms tightly across his chest. *He picks on me*. And no, I didn't realize the extra seat was for him. Doesn't matter. There's plenty of food and wine for everyone. You"—Chase motioned to Rhys—"answer the door. And you"—pointing to Mark—"go entertain your girl and her family. As for me, I'll be in the kitchen." Chase snapped his mouth closed and fled through the kitchen door, hoping Rhys would not follow.

"But the doorbell didn't—" Mark's complaint was cut off by the sudden *ding-dong* of said doorbell.

"Don't ask how he does that," Rhys said. "I'll get the door, since he's the one giving the orders tonight."

Chase heard Rhys move toward the door. An instant later, glasses clinked in the front room and voices he didn't recognize were saying hello. Eternally thankful for interruptions and distractions, Chase continued the final prep for dinner. He caught himself rubbing the palm of his right hand nervously down his thigh, which only served to annoy him more. "Shouldn't react to him like that, dammit!" he swore under his breath.

Every time Rhys's laugh wafted in from the other room, he bit back a groan. Chase hated how his groin tightened and his cock sat up every time. "He's not even *that* cute," he continued to grumble.

Things got weird again when Chase went to serve the first course. Chase sat a shallow bowl of chilled salad before each person, trying to be as unobtrusive as possible. When he sat the dish in front of Aurora's mom, Janet, she stopped him.

"Excuse me, but do you mind if I ask you a question, dear?" Her bright smile put him at ease right away.

"What do you need, ma'am?"

"Such manners! I simply adore your friends, Mark." Turning back to Chase, she continued, "Well, dear, two things. Are you going to join us for dinner, or has Mark roped you into playing server only?"

"Oh, I came over to help him cook a little. This is really his baby," Chase explained, gesturing to the diner he'd just set out. "But, no, I'm not staying. This is a family meal."

Janet smiled slowly and nodded. "I hope to get to meet you again, then. Oh, and I wanted to know about your necklace. It's a bit unusual but very cute."

"My necklace?" Chase thought for a moment about what he was wearing. "Oh! The Spoon Theory choker, you mean?"

"Yes. I don't think I have ever seen a spoon like that for a choker before. Does it mean something special, or is it just something you liked?"

"Actually, it's a sort of hero amulet for my best friend." At the blank looks all around, Chase decided a little more explanation was needed. "Have you heard of 'The Spoon Theory'?" Only Rhys didn't shake his head. "It's a little story about how a person with an invisible or little understood illness or disability has only so much energy, or so many 'spoons' for each day, and how they count each one to make sure they can do all the things they need to do. The problem is, most don't have enough spoons to do everything they have to do, so they have to learn to prioritize or suffer."

Chase stopped and thought about the choker, lost in thought for a moment. It was a little iridescent blue spoon with a stylized JB inside a silver heart. "There's a lot more to it, but my BFF, James, has Ehlers-Danlos syndrome, and he lives his life having to struggle that way. He rarely says anything to anyone about it, though, not even his partner. This is something I wear to remind me of his fight. His initials are engraved on the bowl of the spoon if you look closely," he added, pointing to the choker.

"That's so sweet of you, Chase," Janet commented. "I'd love to look into that story you mentioned, if you would give me the name of the site or where I can get it."

"I'll leave it with Mark, but for now, eat up. Dinner is almost ready." On his way back to the kitchen, Chase caught the thoughtful smile Rhys gave him. It seemed almost affectionate, but that couldn't be right. Rhys had made his opinion quite clear, and besides, he had no interest in the big oaf anyway! *Yeah, right,* a traitorous little voice inside whispered.

RHYS WATCHED Chase maneuver around the dining room, placing the hot plates at each setting. Admiring how good Chase looked in the all-black outfit he wore, he again hated himself for how they'd met and the things he had said. He was really beginning to wonder if pushing Chase away was one of his more stupid mistakes.

He fought not to growl when Mark stood and hugged Chase before he left. It was ridiculous, he knew, but he hated seeing others be able to touch Chase when he couldn't. Shaking Chase's hand earlier had been both bliss and torture. If only he could trust Chase to be the kind of man

James said he was, not the club twink he'd seemed to be when Rhys had first met him.

Aurora's father, Ryan, regarded Rhys with the same knowing smirk his father did at times. Of course, Ryan and his dad being first cousins probably accounted for it, but even so. "You sweet on that one, huh, Rhys?"

"What?" Rhys choked. "No. He's our new computer guy, that's all."

Ryan chuckled dryly. "Son, you could have cut the tension between the two of you with a steak knife. It's the same look your dad used to give your mum when they were teens." He continued to stare at Rhys as he began to eat. "And damn! He can cook too."

"Sir, Chase works for me, so no matter what I may or may not feel, is beside the point," Rhys explained, trying to keep both his voice and stare firm.

Ryan looked over at Mark. "Is he always this obtuse? Or is there a real reason he's not courtin' the boy?"

Mark shrugged. "I haven't been able to get the story out of either of them on why they act like that to each other. *I* think he likes Chase, but then deep down, I think Chase likes him too. Just wish I could figure out why they're not together."

"Oh come on, you two, stop picking on Rhys," Aurora cut in. "I'm sure he has his reasons for not pursuing the cutie. Now, don't be rude, Rhys. Eat up."

Rhys smiled and took his first bite of the meal and this time he did groan. "Damn, he really can cook." He immediately blushed. "I, uh, mean nice?"

Everyone laughed.

As dinner wore on, Rhys mainly kept quiet, preferring to enjoy both the company and the terrific food. He was thankful, though, that Aurora managed to direct the conversation away from the possibility of him and Chase.

Once dinner was over, Rhys excused himself so the couple and her parents could have some unsupervised time together. Mark had only asked him to "supervise" dinner. He reached for the door, but was stopped by a small, soft hand on his arm.

"Can I walk you up, Rhys?" Aurora asked, concern clear in her eyes.

"I only live upstairs, sweetheart." The look in her eyes had him nodding and offering her his arm. "Fine, come lecture me too."

Neither spoke on the way up to Rhys's third-floor loft. Once inside he offered her a drink and the couch. "Soda? Tea?"

"No, Rhys. Now, come here and talk to me a little."

Rhys walked slowly over to sit on the couch beside her, unsure of what she had to say and dreading it all the same.

"I'm not here to lecture you," Aurora began, giving a gentle pat to his big hand. "You should know better. However, I do want to ask you what's wrong. I know your type, and that cute little twink is so your type, it's beyond not funny. So, just curious—what gives? And why did he seem alternatively excited and hurt when he stared at you?"

"Long story, but suffice to say, I acted like a drunk-ass fool the night we met, and any chance between us was pretty much over before I sobered." Rhys looked down, not sure how to ask what he really wanted to know.

"What is it? You've always been my big protector, now let me be your shoulder."

Rhys nodded slowly. "Um, did he really look at me like you and the others said?"

She looked him over and smirked. "You mean, did he look like he either wanted to eat you up or throttle you? Oh, yeah!"

He joined in her laughter. "Fine, little miss bossy, I'll think about it. That's the best I can offer right now. I mean, even if I wanted to, I'm not sure he'd be willing to try. James, the friend he mentioned, is the one that conned him into working for Mark and me in the first place," he explained reluctantly.

chapter four

EVER SINCE the dinner at Mark's, Rhys had been noticing Chase more and more. All the little things he did for Nichelle, like bringing her treats when he came back from his consulting runs, or for Mark… or even for him occasionally. He'd taken the time over the last two weeks to watch how Chase interacted with others and how dedicated he seemed while working, whether for his consulting business or for their agency, and was beyond impressed. Rhys had been skeptical when James and Seth insisted Chase was the right techie, but he was a believer now.

Rhys was startled out of his thoughts by a knock on the door. "Come in."

Chase poked his head around the door. "Nichelle said you needed to see me after your last appointment left?" Chase nibbled his bottom lip, causing the ring to flick and pull against the tantalizing bit of flesh. Damn, but he wanted to taste those lips!

Rhys voice came out rougher than he'd intended. "Yes, come in, please." He motioned to one of the overstuffed chairs in front of his desk. "I need to talk to you about a case, but… it's sensitive."

Chase stared at him for a moment before nodding. "That is what you pay me for, so what do you need?"

Rhys looked him over a moment, unsure how the man would take what he was asking, and again wishing Chase would be his flirty, normal self around him. "I need some surveillance footage gone through. In a few cases, we'll probably need stills captured too. Maybe even sections pieced together for a presentation."

"That shouldn't be hard."

26

He swore Chase's eyes bored holes through him as he continued to explain. "The material is delicate, and what you see, you can't speak of outside these walls. Not even to James."

"I signed your confidentiality agreement, Mr. Sayer," Chase snapped.

"Hey, no getting pissy. I said the same to Kailee early on too."

Chase gave a sort of half smile and nodded. "What exactly am I'm looking at and for?"

"Hold on," Rhys countered. The next part was what he dreaded. "I also need you to dig through a laptop and see what you can pull from it. Passwords for online journals, hidden files, et cetera. Dig as deep as you can to find out if it's possible his apparent suicide might have, in reality, been murder."

Chase gaped at him. "Su-suicide?"

Rhys nodded, hating that he needed to involve Chase in this. He'd never felt guilty for asking such things from Kailee, but from Chase? Yeah, that bothered him for reasons he refused to examine.

Chase swallowed and nodded. "And the footage?"

"It's from the building our possible victim lived in, as well as from a short documentary he was working on. I don't know if anything's on there or not. The police wrote it off as 'gay suicide'," he growled. Rhys had many opinions on suicide, but for it to be dismissed like that made him so angry he wanted to throw something, or maybe pummel anyone able to discount the value of others' lives like that.

He was startled out of his internal fuming by the gentle touch of a cool hand settling over his. "Hey, it's all right, Rhys. If there *is* anything to find, I *will* find it. You do your thing, and I will do mine."

He looked up to find those beautiful blue-and-green eyes gazing softly at him. Between the touch and the look offered, Rhys felt his anger calming and his heart rate slowing. He wasn't sure anyone had ever had that effect on him, but was grateful right then.

"Thanks, Chase. Sorry. Suicide is horrible enough without people making jokes or blowing it off like the person's existence didn't matter."

Chase pulled his hand back slowly, and Rhys wished he would've left it a little longer.

"I know." Chase fidgeted with his wrist cuff and swallowed hard. "I lost a cousin when we were in high school."

The haunted look in Chase's eyes worried him. Rhys thought for a moment. "Are you going to be able to handle this, then?"

Chase quirked a small smile. "Yes. I will. You take a break and then go do your thing." He got up and wandered out of Rhys's office, mumbling, "Hmm, let me see what I can find."

CHASE COULDN'T take watching Rhys move around like he was. The pain and stiffness in his shoulders and neck seemed almost as pronounced as the pain lines around his eyes and lips. He didn't know why Rhys was hurting, but he longed to help, to make him feel a little better, even if only for a few minutes.

Seeing Rhys settle down into one of the large plush chairs in the reception area of the office, Chase decided to swallow his pride and pushed away from his desk and computers. Standing up, he carefully stretched his arms above his head until he felt the release of tension in his back and neck. He then moved slowly over to where Rhys was before lightly clearing his throat.

"Rhys?"

He grunted.

"Look, I know you don't really like me, but would you let me try to help with the pain some?" Chase had no idea if Rhys would agree, but he had to try. As much as he hated to admit it, Rhys was actually a pretty decent guy, even if he was, sadly, biased against guys like him.

"I don't—"

Chase decided to take the decision from Rhys—well, unless he rejected his help. With slow, deliberate motions, Chase stretched his hands to each side of Rhys's head at the same time as he took a step closer. Setting his middle and ring fingers on Rhys's temples, he began to rub in gentle circles.

Rhys tensed but then sighed and relaxed somewhat.

"Here, lean forward a little, and I'll move behind you so I can get to your neck and shoulders." Without waiting, Chase moved behind the chair and gently glided the fingers of his right hand down Rhys's neck to see what, if anything, he could sense about the tension there. He brought his left hand into the caress-like assessment before he began the gentle massage. He didn't put any real force behind the motions at first.

"Relax, Rhys. Get used to my touch, and then I'll add the pressure needed to help you." Chase continued his light massage, increasing the strength used incrementally until he was exerting himself a little. "Seriously, I don't know what's got you so tense, but it hurts to even look at you right now."

Rhys let out a deep, rumbling sound—a cross between a moan and a growl—after a few minutes of the stronger, more demanding massage. "God, you're good at that."

Glad he was behind the chair so Rhys couldn't see the large bulge in his tight jeans, Chase continued to work his neck and shoulder muscles.

"Is this from an injury or something?"

Rhys shook his head slightly and sighed. "No. Just, *ohhh*, stress. Damn, Chase, where did you learn to do *tha-a-at*?"

Chase giggled at the way Rhys was reacting to a little muscle pampering. "When James was hurt years ago in that wreck his ex caused, his physiotherapist wanted him to have a massage after his sessions, but Jamie couldn't stand to let people touch him. His physio taught me how he wanted it done for James."

Rhys's head snapped up. He turned to look at Chase over his shoulder. "You learned massage just to help James?"

"I was about the only person he could stand to have touch him for a long time," Chase explained with a shrug. "He lived with me for a while after he was released from the hospital, since he couldn't walk and had to rebuild his strength and all." He tensed at the strange look Rhys was giving him. "What?"

"He always glosses over any questions about that time in his life, other than to insist you are his best friend and were his only family before he met Seth. It never occurred to me you would go to such lengths to help and support him."

"Jamie's my BFF, Rhys. My touch was all he could manage without cringing, crying, or completely freaking out. I did what he needed me to.

That's what you do for the people you love, right?" he asked, right eyebrow raised.

"Well, yeah. I mean…." Rhys trailed off when the door chimed and opened.

Startled, Chase took a step backward at the venomous look coming from the blond guy sauntering toward him and Rhys.

GODDAMMIT ALL! I do not need this today!

"Garrett," Rhys snapped, his voice cold and hard. "What do you want?"

Ignoring him, Garrett's eyes focused on Chase. "This your new little boy toy, Rhys? Bet we could have some fun playing with him. What do ya think?"

Garrett's voice was sweet, too sweet. And judging by the way Chase moved away from him, and the way he kept looking between him and Garrett, Rhys knew what little peace he had managed with Chase was now gone.

"You're not welcome here, Garrett, and you know it. Now leave," Rhys ground out, stepping between Chase and Garrett.

As much as he hated to, Rhys couldn't completely stop himself from doing a once-over, taking in Garrett's toned body, the painted-on club clothes, how he stood, hip cocked and left thumb hooked in the top of his pants, fingers splayed to draw the eye to his package. Even with everything that had happened, there was still a part of Rhys that wanted Garrett back. Wanted to taste and feel him again, but he quickly pushed those thoughts away, reminding himself why he'd thrown the little slut out months ago. Of course, he was also the reason why Chase thought he didn't like him.

"Oh, babe, this playing-hard-to-get thing is getting old. So, send the little plaything home or back to wherever you found him and let's go upstairs," Garrett cooed with his best come-hither look. "I miss you."

"Office or out! We are not having this conversation here!" Rhys demanded, arms folded across his chest, and he fought not to show how much it hurt seeing Garrett, much less hearing the lies he spouted in front of Chase.

"Mmm… office sex? Kinky!" Garrett called out as he sauntered quickly into Rhys's office.

Rhys looked at Chase, taking in the revulsion and pain in his eyes and hating himself a little more for having put it there. "Please, don't leave. Let me deal with *him*, and I'll…. Just give me a chance to explain things, 'cause I know this looks really bad."

"It's fine," Chase snapped. "You don't owe me anything."

"No, please. I'll be right back. Promise you will still be here."

"Then pray you can finish with your *friend* before I finish packing up my tech. Hurry, you shouldn't keep your *boy* waiting." Chase spun around and stormed off.

Rhys stood frozen for a moment. He'd hurt Chase, again, thanks to Garrett showing up and saying those things to and about him. Worse, Garrett's looks proved Rhys had lied when he'd rejected Chase at the club. *Dammit!*

Rhys sprinted into his office, slamming the door before he turned to Garrett. "I told you to never come back here. To never contact me, talk to me, or even think my name. What in the hell do you want?"

"I miss you, babe," Garrett started, but Rhys cut him off.

"Cut the crap. What. Do. You. Want? You don't miss me. What, your little sugar daddy dumped you so you thought you'd slink back to me? Either way, get out."

"But Rhys, I need you. I bet your new little boy can't do everything for you I can," he purred again, attempting to slide his hand up Rhys's arm.

He slapped the man away. "First off, Chase is not my lover. If he was, unlike you, I would never cheat on him, and especially not with a skank like you. Secondly, you are not welcome here. And finally, I don't love you anymore. Now, get *out!*" Rhys wrenched the door open, right arm pointed toward the front door.

"But—"

"Out!"

Garrett slunk out the door. Rhys followed right behind, flipping the lock and turning over the closed sign the moment Garrett cleared the door. He only hesitated a moment when he heard the slamming and banging coming from the IT area in back. Rhys slowly marched to the rear, hoping he could find a way to mend things with Chase.

It wasn't like they were exactly friends, but he did respect Chase, and God, his dreams were constantly filled with his cravings for the slight man. When he entered the area, he saw Chase already had most of the equipment he had brought in packed up and stacked to the side.

Rhys cleared his throat. "Chase."

Chase spun around; the look on his face made Rhys take a step backward. "Share me? Your new boy toy? Huh, and here I thought you didn't like 'twinks'," he yelled, making air quotes on the last word. "Or is it just me you can't stand for some reason?" Chase flailed his arms as he ranted. "You humiliated me, shunned me, and now...." He snatched up some small objects he kept to toy with when antsy and hurled them as he kept shouting. "Now your boyfriend—one I didn't even know existed—treats me like a sex toy for your mutual amusement!"

Rhys ducked most of the items as each flew at his head—*boy has a damn good arm, wow.* Finally reaching Chase, Rhys grabbed him before anything else could go flying. "Stop, Chase. I know what I said and did that night at the club, and... I'm sorry."

"I don't care if you're sorry. I will not be used by you or anyone else!"

"Chase," Rhys whispered, pulling Chase flush against him. "You've had your turn, now it's mine. Do you think you can stop yelling and throwing things long enough to hear me out?"

"Fine!"

Chase stomped past him toward the front, but as he left behind all his equipment, Rhys had hope, though he was not entirely sure what for. He followed the little man all the way out to the waiting area, where he proceeded to flop down on one of the couches.

Rhys carefully sat across from him. "Chase?"

"What?"

"Look at me, please."

Chase turned toward him, but instead of the silent treatment or yelling, his eyes widened in shock, his mouth forming a silent, horrified O. He seemed positively ill before he finally spoke. "Oh, Rhys. Did I do that?"

"Do what? What are you staring at me like that for?"

"You, you're bleeding," Chase squeaked. Before Rhys could figure out what he was talking about, Chase bolted for the back, returning quickly with the backpack Rhys noticed he always seemed to carry.

Rhys reached up to touch his face but stopped when Chase grabbed his wrist firmly. "No, don't touch. Let me see how bad the cut is."

Surprised at both the strength used and the command in the tone, he sat still, letting Chase fuss and fidget with some kind of cleaning cloth near his right eye. It stung a little but he barely noticed. What he did notice was Chase blowing cool, cinnamon-scented air across the scratch to help soothe the sting.

Without thinking, Rhys moaned in pleasure when Chase traced his fingers along his brow after smoothing a single butterfly closure over the cut. Rhys froze when Chase feathered a barely there kiss across his forehead.

"I'm sorry, Rhys. I didn't mean to lose control like that. I'll go now, okay?"

Chase didn't pull away even after saying he was leaving. Rhys searched his eyes, startled yet drawn in by the mix of desire and confusion swirling within the green-and-blue depths. Before he could stop himself, Rhys leaned forward the tiny amount that separated them and rested his lips against Chase's. He didn't push to deepen the kiss, keeping it chaste, yet it was one of the most wonderful moments of his life.

When Chase still didn't move away, he gently cupped Chase's face, careful not to rush him. After another moment, he flicked his tongue out to slide against Chase's bottom lip, pausing to tease the silver ring that had tantalized him ever since he had first seen Chase wearing it.

Chase gasped, slightly parting his lips, which Rhys took as an invitation to deepen the kiss. Rhys pushed forward, sliding his tongue tentatively past Chase's lips, delving into the moist heat of his mouth, tasting cinnamon but with an earthy, addictive essence that was all Chase.

He was so hard he could barely think past *more* and *God, yes, please.*

chapter five

HIS BACK against the wall, Rhys gasped and struggled to process what had just happened. Chase pinned him in place with nothing more than a look and a growl. When Chase pulled Rhys's head down, he smelled the faint puffs of cinnamon-scented breath as they ghosted over his face. Along with the Antaeus Chase always wore, it almost brought him to his knees.

Chase slid his hand up to tangle his fingers in Rhys's shoulder-length hair. He pulled sharply, eliciting a gasp from Rhys. "For tonight, only you and I exist. We do things my way or not at all. Your body is mine. Your pleasure is mine. Am I understood?"

Unprepared for Chase taking control in such a way, all he could manage was a small nod. Rhys had fantasized about Chase many times, but had always made sure to keep his walls up between them. Right then, he couldn't remember why. For such a diminutive man, his dominance and strength had Rhys's cock diamond-hard and throbbing where it sat trapped in his jeans.

Chase touched his lips against Rhys's, but the hold he had on Rhys's hair kept him from moving into the touch. "I need to hear you, Rhys," Chase murmured against his lips.

"Please" was all Rhys could manage.

"Your place is upstairs, right?" Chase paused until Rhys nodded. "Then lead the way," he added, then stepped back suddenly and motioned that he would follow.

The sudden loss of Chase's warmth and touch caused a physical ache in his chest he was too afraid to investigate right then—or possibly ever. Rhys went up the private stairs to his third-floor loft, so overwhelmed with lust and fear he could barely manage the lock to let them both inside.

Before he could close the door all the way, hands grabbed him, spinning and slamming him against the door. He opened his mouth in surprise, but couldn't get out the question in his mind as Chase once again manhandled him, pulling his head down to deliver a punishing kiss. One so mind-melting, he trembled and moaned into the kiss. Rhys was so caught up in the near-brutal plunder of his mouth, the pain of teeth mashing against lips welcomed and needed. When he suddenly felt small but strong hands slide up his pecs, caressing and kneading, he pushed into the sensations and sucked hard on Chase's wicked tongue. Chase traced down his abs, rubbing and teasing Rhys's muscles as he moved lower.

"Off," Chase snapped, tugging on the hem of Rhys's shirt once he broke the kiss.

In a daze, Rhys stood up enough to lift his shirt over his head.

He moaned again when he felt a hot mouth cover one nipple, sucking and licking it into a swollen nub. "Oh God!" he yelled when Chase pinched the other hard while continuing his assault on his first nipple. After another moment, Chase switched, soothing the pinch with his tongue before licking and sucking it, hard, into his mouth.

"Like that?"

"You have no idea," he groaned.

Chase chuckled. Rhys couldn't decide if it sounded more delighted or evil, but couldn't bring himself to care.

"Bed? You're too tall to do what I want with you still standing up."

Rhys's mind swam, contemplating what all that might entail as he hurried to lead Chase to his bedroom.

"Nice bed, big guy. Now, stop where you are. First, is there anything I should know?"

Rhys shook his head. "I'm neg."

"Good, so am I. We're still going to play safe, though. Supplies?"

"Nightstand."

"Cool."

Chase leaned back in, licking and kissing his way down Rhys's body, tracing just under the waistband of his jeans. *A little lower, please,* Rhys silently begged.

Chase's tongue flicked into his belly button at the same time he felt smooth, nimble hands quickly unbutton and unzip his fly, finally freeing his weeping, needy rod. Chase suddenly dropped to the floor, ripping Rhys's jeans down to his ankles. The warmth that enveloped his head as Chase mouthed the tip through his boxers required him to fight gravity, his knees threatening to buckle as they shook.

"Mmm… need more of that." Chase groaned and pulled down Rhys's boxers until both items hobbled him and cool air kissed his wet cock. Chase's tongue lapped at him as he moved down his member, suddenly burying his nose in his balls. Warm wetness encased one ball, then the other, as Chase laved and sucked each in turn. A slender hand wrapped around his cock, giving a couple of hard, tight pumps before both mouth and hand left him so suddenly, Rhys shifted forward before his mind could catch up.

His gaze locked with Chase's. Chase helped him out of the remainder of his clothes. Rhys stretched out one trembling hand to touch Chase's soft, spiky hair but froze when, instead of allowing the touch or moving away from him, Chase plunged down onto his length, licking, sucking, and vibrating his cock with moans that had him thrusting into the hottest, most demanding mouth that had ever touched him. Rhys liked blowjobs, giving and receiving, but no one had made him feel like this before.

Rhys was desperate with need, and his balls tightened and drew up. Tapping on Chase's shoulder, he choked out, "Stop. I'm gonna…. Oh…."

Despite the attempted warning, Chase redoubled his efforts and a moment later a wet finger ghosted back across his taint and began to tap at his rosy opening. Shock spread through him with every tap and after only a few more, he lost his hold, bellowing and arching as he emptied down Chase's throat.

Rhys watched in a daze as Chase licked him clean, kissed the tip, then stood with a wicked grin on his lips. "Delicious and loud. Mmmm…. Now, on the bed, facedown in the middle."

Rhys hovered at the edge of the bed, trying desperately to process everything. He opened his mouth to speak but found it covered. "No talking. Now, lie down and remember, your body and your pleasure are mine tonight. You won't top tonight, not even from the bottom."

This wasn't how things were supposed to go... and what does he mean, "top from the bottom"? No one he had ever met had taken control from him so fast, seducing and conquering him so thoroughly. As Rhys climbed on the bed and settled into the middle, he couldn't help but tense as he wondered just exactly what Chase had planned next. He was certain Chase wasn't even close to done yet.

Rhys tensed when he heard Chase open and rummage through his "play" drawer. His worry turned to confusion when Chase left the room for a moment. Before he could clear the mix of lust and bliss from his mind, Chase was back. He felt the bed dip beside him and turned to look, confused when he realized Chase was still dressed, other than his feet.

"Stretch out for me, Rhys. Reach up and grab the headboard."

Fingertips trailed down his arms to his shoulders and then up and down his spine. "Rest your head, big guy. Relax."

"Ha-ha. What are you going to do, Chase?"

"Anything and everything I choose to, and you're going to accept it all," Chase purred as he nuzzled Rhys's ear.

Between the smirk in Chase's voice and the purring, Rhys was almost surprised that not only was he hard again already, but he wasn't actually sure if his cock had ever gone down any in the first place. He'd never rebounded so fast in his life, not even when he was a teenager! His arousal and the ache in his rim excited him more with each thought of what Chase might do to him.

Chase slid his still fully clothed body onto Rhys's naked one. Chase's slight weight settled across his upper thighs and buttocks firmly, the rough texture of jeans abrading the sensitive flesh they touched. Chase stretched out against him, covering him as he slowly kissed and nibbled up his spine, startling a gasp from him that turned into a deep moan when he bit hard at the tender skin where shoulder meets neck and ground his denim-clad cock against Rhys's crack at the same time.

When Chase released Rhys's shoulder, quickly licking away the sting, he fought for a moment of clarity, annoyed at how wanton and weak his behavior was—like Chase could really hold him down and make him submit!

This is completely insane. "I don't… I haven't… um.…" *Not for a very, very long time….*

"Shh… big guy. I'll take good care of you, I promise." Chase shifted up on his knees again, rocking his erection against Rhys's ass.

It wasn't that he feared Chase abusing him. He simply couldn't believe his reaction to the sexiest little twink boy he had ever seen. The sound of a top snapping open brought him fully back to the present, and he braced himself for what Chase would do to him. He wasn't completely certain he could do this, but God he wanted to, wanted to feel Chase fill him as he had been only a few times in his thirty-two years.

"Relax, Rhys. You've already felt the worst pain I'm likely to ever deliver," Chase said, touching the spot he'd bitten.

Rhys worked to focus and release some of the tension in his body, then nodded to show Chase he'd heard and understood him.

After a moment, oil-slicked hands slid up his back, working on the knotted muscles and pains throughout it and his neck. Chase worked him like he had that first time, powerful yet gentle at the same time. It was so sensual and tender; he was torn between grinding back into Chase and sighing. He was a little disappointed when Chase shifted off him, but bit the inside of his cheek to stop the grunt that fought to be expressed. Rhys heard the cap snap again, and then strong fingers worked his calves and thighs. The hands left again, but only for the briefest moment, and returned dried to caress and massage his cheeks in such a way as to repeatedly expose his nearly virgin opening.

"Raise up for me a minute," Chase purred, shoving a pillow under Rhys's hips when he did as commanded.

Again the hands kneaded and separated his cheeks, and then a steady stream of cool air tickled his opening before Chase licked a wide path from the base of his balls to the top of his crack. Rhys tensed when Chase swept over his hole, but he didn't stop there, continuing to the top before starting again at his balls. Chase made a couple of runs like that before focusing on Rhys's tight, damp opening. He alternated between licks, nibbles, and blowing cool air across the heated, wet skin. When Chase finally added pointed stabs with the tip of his tongue to the pattern, Rhys was already writhing, begging, and pushing himself back against Chase's face, though he couldn't seem to articulate more than *please* or *more* as he trembled and cried out.

The mind-numbing assault stopped just as quickly as it had begun, leaving him teetering on the edge of what he felt would probably be the best orgasm of his life, drawing out a growl of aching frustration. Rhys was about to demand Chase get his happy little ass back to work and let him come again, when he realized he was alone on the bed.

The soft rustle of fabric shifting and landing on the floor calmed his frayed nerves and allowed him to grasp enough patience to wait for Chase to continue. The sight of a condom landing beside him as Chase moved back behind him was reassuring, both because Chase had remembered—since a few moments before Rhys wouldn't have cared if they used one or not—and because it meant Chase was *finally* getting to the whole fucking part. Never in his life had he gotten so carried away he'd forgotten about a rubber. Not until Chase started touching him that is.

One more time, Rhys heard the snick of a cap popping, but this time he knew it was the lube, not the massage oil. He shifted his legs wider apart, hoping to hurry Chase up, tipping his ass up a little in silent offering. When a finger finally touched him, he nearly cried in relief. Two fingers circled his now eager hole, tickling and massaging a bit before one slender digit was carefully pushed past his rim and guardian muscles. Chase paused, letting him adjust to the intrusion, though he would have been happier not to delay any more. Once that finger started pumping in and out, twisting as it moved, Rhys was right back to being on edge again, pushing back on Chase's finger.

"Another, please, Chase."

A soft giggle met his ears as a second finger joined the first, sliding in and out, scissoring him open. When a third finger pushed in, he tensed, the burn flaring from the amount of stretching—the penetration something he almost never allowed and hadn't done in ages. The sting was quickly forgotten when those skilled fingers curled and started tagging his gland with every thrust.

The fingers disappeared, and he heard the wrapper tearing, and then Chase was flush against him once more. The head of Chase's cock was right at his opening, teasing him as it tapped against him; just a little push and he would slide into him.

"Are you sure you want this, Rhys? I know I said I was in charge, but I would never force or coerce you into more than you truly want to give."

Rhys whimpered. "Now? You ask me now? Fuck me, damn it! Please!"

A slight weight shift behind him, and suddenly he was being breached. The feeling of being stretched and filled was excruciatingly erotic because of how slow and careful Chase was with him. Once fully seated, Chase stopped, holding still as he pressed tightly against him until Rhys pushed back. But instead of withdrawing to slide back in, Chase pushed harder, until Rhys's thoughts shut down altogether. When Chase did move, it was to snap his hips forward, without drawing back, jabbing so deep within him Rhys was certain he would be feeling this for days. Weeks, maybe. He had never been taken like this, or even thought of it. The jackhammer-like thrusts rubbed the length of Chase's cock against his gland each time, and deeper than he'd imagined possible.

"Please. I gotta... I need...." Rhys gasped, not knowing anything other than the need to come and the brain-numbing desire for Chase to come with him.

Chase shifted, and instead of the deep jabs, he began pounding in, sliding almost all the way out, then driving in again, one hand buried in Rhys's hair, tugging hard enough to pull him up, arching his back. Rhys increased his hold on the headboard spindles, savoring the friction and power Chase used.

"Come for me, Rhys. I want to feel you milk me dry!"

Rhys couldn't have stopped his orgasm if his life depended on it. With a scream that seemed to tear loose from somewhere deep inside him, he slammed into Chase and came. A split second later, Chase faltered as he thrust, groaning his completion right behind Rhys's own.

By the time he could focus again, Chase was kneeling beside him, pushing on his hip. "Come on, big guy. Turn on your side for me."

Rhys turned, but that was about all the energy he seemed to have. Before he could ask why, though, he felt a damp cloth cleaning him from abs to the top of his ass. The pillow was moved away and a sheet draped over him. With a heavy sigh, he opened his eyes again, taking his first look at Chase naked, and nearly stopped breathing. He was... beautiful!

And hung, though his ass had already let him in on that little—or not so little—fact.

"I wasn't too rough on you, was I?" Chase asked, his voice soft and tender, more so than usual.

"No. Wonderful," Rhys mumbled, his words slurring slightly.

Chase smiled. The kiss Chase gave him was sweet, like what he thought a first kiss should be. "Sleep now. Nothing else exists until morning."

The last thing Rhys knew was the light caress of Chase's fingers against his arm and the gentle whisper of Chase's breath against his chest.

CHASE LAY awake, watching Rhys sleep, pain and regret filling him. He knew he'd just lost a piece of his heart to a man who, deep down, could never love him. Never truly respect him. Hell, Rhys hadn't even really been with him; he'd called another man's name as he came the second time.

How he'd let things get so out of hand, he had no clue, but with tears in his eyes and guilt eating his heart, he quietly slipped out of bed. Dressing as quickly and quietly as possible, he fled Rhys's home, swearing he would find another tech person to help Rhys's company as soon as possible.

How he could face Rhys after what had just happened, he didn't know. But resolved to his fate—he was no man's trick or placeholder—he drove home and cried himself to sleep.

chapter six

CHASE WOKE with a start. The sound of banging, then locks clicking, brought him out of the fitful sleep he'd been trapped in since he'd finally cried himself out. Still fully clothed, having crashed on the bed as he was when he'd fled Rhys's the night before, he reached for the baseball bat he always kept by the nightstand, hoping it was just James using his key.

"He probably just overslept, pet. You know he goes out clubbing with some of his other friends." Seth's deep voice was soft, soothing.

"No, Seth. He's not answering his cell. Simon and the others haven't seen him today, and he didn't go out with them last night. It's after three in the afternoon, yet he was supposed to meet me at ten. So where is he?" That was James's voice, but it was high and tight like it only got when he was scared.

Chase rounded the corner to find his best friend, James, and James's fiancé, Seth Burns, heading straight for his bedroom.

"James? Seth?" Chase croaked. His voice was tight and scratchy, probably from the pointless crying the night before, or had it been earlier this morning? "What are you doing here?"

"Chase!" James cried, flinging himself down the short hall as fast as he could with his forearm crutches.

Chase released the bat and soon had his arms full of James. He looked past James to Seth, and with a weak voice asked, "What are you guys doing here, and why is he freaking out?"

"Five hours, Chase! That's how long ago you were supposed to be at the studio to meet me. The private sitting was today, remember? Seth doesn't like me to be alone with strangers in my studio, so you said you'd be there, but you never showed. Your cell goes straight to voice mail. Simon, Dale, Vaughn—no one has heard from you all day," James rattled off, practically in one breath.

He could feel the pressure of Seth rubbing up and down James's back as he held him.

"Calm down, hun. I'm right here, safe and sound. I just—" Chase bit off his words, having no idea how to explain why he hadn't been where he was supposed to be.

James suddenly pushed him back, holding tight to his arms, looking him up and down with a curious expression on his handsome face. He cupped Chase's cheeks, the tenderness of the motion nearly breaking his heart again. "Chase, what's wrong?"

"Nothing for you to worry about. I just had a rough night." Looking past James to Seth, he murmured, "Can you get him settled? I'll shower and be right out. I really am very sorry for upsetting you both."

"James, come on. Let's go sit down and wait for Chase," Seth soothed, handing James's crutches to him again.

Chase mouthed "thank you" to Seth before he fled to his room.

After a quick shower to get the scent of Rhys and sweat off, Chase quickly dressed in a simple T-shirt and a pair of old, threadbare jeans he kept for bumming around in. He didn't feel up to much right then, but he reckoned more than sleep pants would be good, considering Seth was with James. Otherwise, he wouldn't have worried about even that much.

After popping a couple of Tylenol, Chase headed out to find where his company was. He got as far as his kitchen, where he found not only James and Seth, but a mug of his favorite blonde roast coffee waiting for him.

"Thanks," he offered, his voice soft. He wasn't sure he had the energy for the coming conversation, but he would never turn James away, not even now.

All three men entered the living room, where Chase flopped into his favorite chair, giving James and Seth the couch.

"Chase," James started tentatively. "What happened to you last night? Who hurt you?"

"What makes you think someone hurt me? I'm fine, just tired."

James leaned forward, his face turning hard. "I know it was a guy that put you in this mood, Chase. My nose works just fine, and you, dear," he continued, wrinkling his nose, "you smelled of sex when we got here. And, well, you look so sad. I didn't even know you were dating someone, but whoever he is, he's obviously not good enough for you if he hurt you." James finished with a snort.

A slight smile tugged at his lips for a moment. God, he loved his BFF. Who else could call you out on having sex, snort, and insult an unknown man all in one breath?

"Jamie, I'm not dating anyone, so there is nothing to tell. I wasn't holding out on you."

"Ha! Don't give me that crap. You don't have one-night stands. You go clubbing, dance, and even hit on guys, but you never go home with any of them, so try again," James snapped, his eyes almost as hard as his voice.

"Really?" Seth asked.

"God!" Chase barked, throwing his hands up. "Why does everyone think I'm a damn slut? Yes, really, Seth. If I take someone to bed, it's after we've gotten to know one another a bit and I have real feelings for the person. Why is—never mind. The point, Jamie, is that no, I'm not dating anyone, and I'd really rather never see the person from last night again."

Merely saying that much felt like picking at a not-quite-formed scab. Ignoring his abandoned mug, Chase rubbed his temples, trying to forget it was the same motion that had started everything with Rhys in the first place.

"Chase, yelling will not help. I only ask because of how you acted when James and I first started seeing one another. My apologies for making assumptions about you. If you aren't seeing anyone, but you had sex and are now upset"—Seth's voice dropped low, hard—"did someone attack you?"

James tensed, and Chase knew he had to stop the panic attack before it set in.

"No, Seth. I just let things get out of hand. Rhys didn't hurt me like that." Chase slapped his hand over his mouth as if he could contain the words that had already slipped out. "Forget I said that last part, please," he cried.

"Rhys? As in our friend and bodyguard Rhys? But...." James's voice trailed off. The mixed look of anger and confusion was not any better than the panic from before, in Chase's opinion.

"Well, Chase is Rhys's type, James. I could see him being interested, but I do not understand how the way the two of you acted before turned into sex, with you this upset after. Rhys would not force you," Seth added with certainty.

Chase groaned loudly. "Please, just forget I said his name. I will find someone else to work for him, and you will simply have to accept that I won't be around when he is if I can help it. Now, please, please, please, drop it," he begged, silently trying to will the two in front of him to listen for once—not that he held much hope of it working.

"I can't do that, Chase. Now, tell me why you need to back out of our agreement and what Rhys did to you to make you so upset? I mean, I know you don't usually do one-offs, but...."

RHYS AWOKE in increments, the sun pushing his consciousness to the surface against his will. His face was buried in the pillow he held crushed to his chest. Rhys pleasantly noted that it smelled of Antaeus and Chase. The memory of the night before had him hard and aching again before he opened his eyes. Rhys reached out, raising his head to look for Chase, hoping to entice the fiery little man into an encore, but the sheets were cold and empty beside him.

When he shifted to sit up and look around, his body reminded him of what he had allowed Chase to do to him. It had been years since he'd done anything but top—more than a decade, he thought. Sliding back down, Rhys drifted his right hand down his chest and abs to his cock as the night before played in his head. The way he'd kissed. The complete and heart-stopping way Chase had possessed his body. Rhys couldn't remember ever being with someone so sensual or caring. It wasn't just the ecstasy, but the massage and time spent prepping him, the cleanup afterward. Everything combined made waking up alone so crushing.

Chase had been angry, but when the fire turned to passion, he'd thought Chase had accepted his apology and wanted him too. Before he got too maudlin, he wondered if maybe Chase hadn't ditched him as just another trick. Maybe something had happened…. But no, he would have woken if a phone had rung.

Rhys forced himself to get out of bed. He first went to his jeans to dig out his cell, a little disappointed to find Chase had left nothing behind. Well, except the used condom in the trash can.

Rhys stood, naked, in the middle of his bedroom as he scrolled through his contacts to find Chase's number. It went straight to voice mail, though, killing the last hope it wasn't really what it looked like.

"Should have known 'Nothing else exists until morning' meant he would be gone when I woke," Rhys muttered as he headed to the bathroom to wash up and get dressed. Before he put on his shirt, he took a moment to look in the mirror and admire the rather clean bite marks at the juncture of neck and shoulder and the other darker little love bites and fingertip bruises.

Rhys took one long, last look at his mussed bed, unable to bring himself to change the sheets and make the bed quite yet. He finished getting dressed and headed down to the office. What met him there was both amusing and annoying. Mark stood in the tech area Chase had set up, staring wide-eyed at both the stacked items and the mess made when Chase had pelted him with all the loose items.

"What the hell, Rhys?" Mark asked, his voice so incredulous Rhys fought to not laugh.

"That would be the effect of Garrett stopping by and pissing Chase off." He absentmindedly touched the bites on his shoulder, remembering the fire in Chase's eyes as he'd shown his displeasure.

"Garrett was here? I thought you swore not to take the slut back!"

"I didn't take him back. Ass. He stopped by to talk to me, trying to convince me he wanted us together again. I threw him out, but not before he called Chase my boy toy, among other things. Chase, um, took exception to that and to how Garrett looked," Rhys added with a shrug. He knew he deserved Chase's anger for the lies and mistreatment, even if he sorely regretted his actions now.

"How he looked? Do I want to know, Rhys?" Mark stooped and started to pick up the scattered items, as did Rhys. "I never understood why you liked him to begin with, but they're both twinks, so what's the problem?"

"You remember I met Chase before we got the contract with Seth to guard James and Danni?" He waited for Mark to nod. "I blew Chase off at a club and insulted him for being a twink. In my defense, it was right after I threw Garrett out, but…."

"You never told Chase the truth, so when the slut stopped by, you looked like a liar on top of being a total ass. Way to go, Rhys."

"I know. Believe me, I know. But he stopped packing up his things and let me apologize."

"You better hope you didn't just cost us the best tech we've ever had. Kailee was good, but Chase really is as good as James said."

"He didn't stay mad, Mark," Rhys said defensively as flashes from the night before again flickered through his mind.

"What'd ya do to your shoulder? You keep messing with it." Mark quirked an eyebrow at him. "And what's with the weird—"

Rhys slapped his hand over the marks he knew were partly visible with only his T-shirt on. *Dammit, knew I shoulda put my jacket on before I came down.* "It's nothing. Don't you have something to do?"

"Uh-uh, let me see," Mark demanded as he grabbed Rhys's shoulder. The wide grin told Rhys Mark already knew what he would find, much to his irritation.

After wrestling for a few minutes, Rhys pinned Mark. "Forget it. I'm not explaining what's there, Mark."

"Spoilsport. Fine, I need to go prep for tonight anyway." He stood when Rhys released him and scowled. "I hate cheating spouse cases," Mark muttered as he stomped off to his office.

Rhys did too, but money was money, and bills didn't care what kind of job was used to pay them.

RHYS LAY sprawled across the top step of his back porch later that evening. He looked across the backyard of his house-slash-business, taking in all the little details he and Mark had put into the place. Most people never saw more than the front office, but the back was a lush area with paths, and plants and flowers when it was warm. Not right then, of course, thanks to the dry, cold weather, but he could still envision what it would look like again come spring.

The cold beer in his hand was probably warmer than the outside temperature, but Rhys didn't care. He had to think, and to do that he needed space that didn't spark memories from the night before. He had been both wrong and right about Chase, though he wasn't sure which bothered him more. The man was beyond his dreams and fantasies in bed, but was either hostile to him or ignored him completely outside it. He knew the latter was his own fault for not 'fessing up about why he'd acted like such a douche at the club. That didn't explain why Chase had run in the middle of the night or why he'd refused both calls and texts.

He wanted to believe the sweet, protective man he had witnessed with James during the stalking was the true person inside, but the clubbing, flamboyant attitude when he didn't know Rhys was there made him doubt. However, Chase leaving before dawn kept the fear that he was merely a notch on Chase's bedpost very fresh and real.

"Rhys!" The strange voice startled him out of his musings. What was he doing here, now?

"'Round back, Jay," Rhys called out. He stood and headed around to the side to open the gate, having recognized James's voice.

A huge smile spread across his face. *Maybe James can help make Chase make sense....*

He paused when he saw James wasn't alone. With him were Simon and Dale, two of Chase's other close friends. It wasn't the extra company that had him worried, but rather the angry scowls each man wore as they approached.

"Um, guys, what can I do you for?" The three men didn't physically intimidate Rhys, but something was obviously wrong, and that bugged him. He didn't know Simon or Dale well, having met them only once or twice, but James was different. "You want to come in?"

James nodded, his body held tight, though a slight tremble showed in his hands as they gripped the crutches he always used. "Please."

Rhys let the three into the enclosed back porch and over to a set of chairs. James settled into one of the cushioned lawn chairs, but Simon and Dale stood, one to each side, as if guarding him—an odd concept in Rhys's opinion, considering he had been James's bodyguard not that long ago.

"First, this is not an attack, Rhys, though I do realize it probably looks like one to you. But after seeing Chase earlier, you have to know why we're upset." James's tone was level but had an unusual edge. James almost never lashed out, so this was a wee bit bizarre, at least to Rhys's knowledge.

"We," Simon added, motioning to himself and Dale, "have a more… hostile opinion of you."

"Okay." Rhys drew the word out. "I have no idea what Chase said to get the three of you upset, but could you tell me why you are here? Please," he quickly added. *What the hell did Chase tell them? I'm the one with marks from last night, not Chase!*

"Using Chase is not cool, man," Simon snapped.

"Use? He said I used him?" Rhys looked back and forth between them, dumbfounded and hurt by the accusation. His shoulders fell at the thought. He was the one feeling used and discarded—the very reason he'd sworn off clubbing twinks, no matter how sexy, until the night before.

The look of confusion that befell the three men before him gave him pause.

"He's ready to quit and try to work it out so he doesn't have to be around when you are. He doesn't want to make me choose between the two of you," James explained, his brows pulled together and lips pursed.

Dale leaned down to James. "Maybe we should ask him his version of last night before we totally condemn the man."

Rhys, still standing with arms folded over his chest, let out a deep breath. "If you know Chase's side of things, no matter what I feel about him sharing such intimate details of our time together, it seems only fair I get to know what he thinks happened too."

chapter seven

CHASE SHIFTED and stretched in his seat, desperate to stay awake for class. He still couldn't believe Dal had convinced him to go back to college for more computer classes. He had his degree already. He was only twenty-six, but looking around the room as it began to fill made him feel old again.

After a few minutes, Chase pulled out his notebook, class book, and favorite pen in a bid not to doze off. He knew better than to go out so soon after the whole debacle with Rhys, but it had made perfect sense to him last night. Or at least Simon had made going out on a blind date seem reasonable.

Before he knew it, Adrian Keys, his professor, was standing at the lecture stand to the right of the large teacher's desk. Tonight they had a special event of sorts; another class was joining theirs for the evening lecture. Something about differing points of view or something. Personally, he couldn't wait to see how the new kids reacted to his hot prof.

Adrian calmly raised his right hand and called out, "Attention, please. My name is Adrian Keys. I will be your instructor this evening." What caught Chase's attention again was how beautiful the man was. Tall—well, taller than him—with hair so black it was almost blue, and eyes such a vibrant green they seemed to burn. As always, what he noticed after that was the unusual tenor of his voice. It was deep, kind of sexy, but also somewhat muted and flat in places. "And this gentleman," he continued, "is Kelley, my feisty assistant. And, while I may not be able to hear what you say, I read lips and"—Adrian's eyes twinkled as he smirked—"Kelley hears everything."

Kelley proceeded to hand out packets to everyone as Adrian continued with his introductory speech. "This is an advanced course. It is also accelerated, so I expect everyone to actively participate and learn all you can from the lecture and each other." Adrian Keys continued to explain what they would learn over the course of the evening. Honestly, it was more of a miniconference, but who was Chase to nitpick over how they named things. Adrian stopped partway when two of the new girls kept chatting while he was lecturing.

"Excuse me, ladies, but if you are not going to participate in the class, you may leave and accept a zero for today."

Chase shifted in his chair, as did most everyone, to stare at the two girls, who blushed and looked away from every eye on them. "But he can't hear!" one of the girls whined.

"No, but I can see. Now choose. Stay and learn, or leave and lose out?"

Glad he wasn't the one those piercing green eyes flashed on, Chase turned his attention back to the man at the front of the room.

As he approached Adrian Keys at the end of the conference-class thing, Chase smiled. "Mr. Keys," he signed, glad to have learned ASL in college—it had seemed logical, given one of his aunts married the sweetest man who happened to be deaf. Besides, he'd never been good with spoken languages. "I need your signature on this form, please. It verifies I am taking the computer forensics class and that I attended this special lecture."

A beatific smile spread across Adrian's face. "Mr. Chase, right?"

"Chase is my first name. Manning is my last."

"Chase then," Adrian signed, then accepted the form and looked it over. "Police consultant? They have a department for this already, yes?"

"Yes, but I have been contracted a couple of times, and it would be better if I had paper proof of all my skills for when they go to the DA or trial," Chase explained and shrugged. Now that he was stuck helping Rhys, this would be even more important. Though he had hoped to get out of working for *that man,* he had instead ended up taking over part of the back office of the Coiled Dragon to house the agency's tech area and his IT consulting firm. He still could not believe Mark had talked him into it, but the man was almost as persuasive as Simon was.

Chase was pulled out of his rambling thoughts when Adrian waved his hand in front of him. "This your only class?"

"No, I have one other. Its last session is tomorrow night."

Adrian again gave him the sweet, open smile that enchanted him every time he saw it. After signing the slip, he handed it back to Chase. "Glad to have you in the class and hope to see more of you." His eyes dropped, and he blushed lightly before he turned and hurried over to Kelley. Chase grinned to himself. *Cute and bashful, yum!*

ALMOST TWO weeks later, Chase found himself back on campus. The same day grades officially posted, he showed up at Adrian's office door. He'd been sort of lusting after the man since the course began, and he had decided the best way to get over Rhys was to find someone new to focus his interest and time on.

Adrian looked up from the papers on his desk, eyebrows raised, head canted slightly to the right. "Chase? How can I help you?" he signed and spoke.

Chase flashed his best smile. "Since you're not my teacher anymore, I wanted to ask if you would like to grab a bite or a beer with me sometime?"

He had to fight not only the nerves from asking Adrian out, but also the distinct, uneasy feeling that his going out with someone was somehow cheating on Rhys—not that he was in a relationship with the big, lumbering, gorgeous man.

Adrian's eyes flashed with an emotion so fast he wasn't sure he could identify it… surprise, maybe. "I'm not sure that would be appropriate, Chase. You are my student."

"Actually, no, I'm not. I *was*, but grades are out, and I don't have you for any classes next term." Chase again tried a smile, hoping it would work this time. He wasn't used to having to work hard to get a first date, but his confidence had been a little shaky since Rhys. Between that and his last couple of dates being duds, his nerves were all twisted up as he awaited Adrian's response.

Adrian took a moment to reply, using the time to slowly look Chase over. A shy smile spread across his handsome face as he nodded. "I would like that."

CHASE STRODE into the office the next morning, his mind more on his upcoming date with Adrian than on the work planned for the day, but he knew once he settled in his chair and booted up everything, he'd descend into the work like always. Whether he was tracking things down for Mark or Rhys or working on the codes for his freelance work, computers were where he ruled, and he loved them.

Working the suicide-or-maybe-murder case still took part of his time and energy, but at least Mark had agreed to work with him on it, reducing the amount of time he had to directly deal with Rhys.

He paused when he spotted something out of place at his workstation. There, beside his favorite keyboard and mouse, was an arrangement of bamboo in a blue-and-green glazed container. Chase quickly counted: seven stalks, two of which were taller, spiraling ones. Set in the pebbles at the base was a small Welsh-style red dragon figurine.

Every morning since the first workday after his and Rhys's "mistake"—as he insisted upon calling their one night together—there had been something peculiar left in his area. A brownie. One of his favorite coffee drinks. Even a new six-pack of Mountain Dew in the minifridge he'd added to his personal area—but plants were new. Chase knew who was leaving them, though he couldn't quite work out why. Rhys baffled and annoyed him, yet he couldn't get their one night or the taste of the man out of his head, no matter what he tried.

Chase moved the plant away, sighed, and then moved it back into view moments later. Giving the little dragon one last look while his system booted up, he turned and dove into his work. He already had a number of clients, and now that he had proper office space, he seemed to be more productive—code and numbers never confused or failed him. The work consumed Chase's thoughts and attention the way it always did.

SOME DAYS a number of people came and went from the office, while other days it was only the four of them.

Lost in his musings and code, he startled when a voice broke into his concentration. "Hey, Chase. You ready to go?"

Looking up, blinking his eyes a few times to refocus on the real world, not his screens, he took in Dal, Rhys's little brother—though not that little. Days like today, with Dal decked out in his police uniform, the three inches Rhys had on him seemed even less noticeable.

Why couldn't it be Dal that makes me squirm and want?

"Um, did I forget something again?" He knew it was things like this that gave him such a rep for being an airhead, but he couldn't help how engrossed he got at times. He was just as focused when playing, so it couldn't all be bad. Right?

Dal's rich laugh made him smile. "Boy, you asked me to stop by on my lunch break so you could pick up your bike, remember? Something about not having time tonight thanks to your pretty little ass having a date," Dal explained, his grin so wide it lit up his entire being.

Chase could feel the heat in his cheeks and looked away. "Yeah, Adrian liked my bike the one time he saw it, and it's our first date, so I...."

"You want to impress the guy. I get it. But I don't have a long break today, so let's go."

He hit "save," then shut things down, grabbed his wallet, keys, and coat, and joined Dal. Dal slid his arm over Chase's shoulders, guiding him to the front.

"Bye, Nichelle."

"Bye, Nikki. It was great seeing you again," Dal added before they exited the office into the chilly, early-afternoon light.

"You two must have been a hot couple, with all her soft mocha skin and your pale skin with the little toffee freckles," Chase mused out loud as he slid into the passenger seat of Dal's cruiser.

"I always thought she was," Dal replied. "But we make much better friends than lovers. Have you met her husband? He's pretty cool."

"Yeah, he was nice when I met him, and cute too," Chase added with a grin.

"You should see his brother. He's even hotter."

Chase did a double take as he stared at Dal. Some het people were open-minded and such, but "hot" and the way his voice had dropped a little when he said it? "And you would know this how? Besides, I am not going to take advice on who's sexy from a straight guy," Chase taunted, waving his hand to push away such a silly thought.

Dal's amused laugh confused Chase even more. "Who said I was straight?"

"But, well… aren't you? I mean, you dated Nichelle. You had just broken up with some girl right before we met at James's, so yeah… straight."

"So, you're one of those gay guys that thinks the whole world is either gay or straight?"

Chase thought that over carefully, considering the harsher tone in Dal's voice. "Well, no. But I've never heard you mention an ex that wasn't female, so I assumed that meant you were het."

"There's this little thing between the two extremes, Chase. I'm bi. And no, that does not mean I'm confused or unsure or finding myself. I happen to be attracted to both women and men."

"I'm sorry, Dal. I didn't mean it that way, honest. I didn't know, is all. Forgive me," he pleaded, batting his eyes as they pulled up to the garage.

"Of course. Now, let's get your bike so you can impress what's his name."

"Adrian, Adrian Keys." He giggled as he thought about the upcoming evening.

"He must really be something if you're giggling. I'm really glad what happened with you and Rhys hasn't stopped you from looking for your Mr. Right."

Chase stood, frozen, as what Dal said washed over him. He was already fighting inexplicable guilt for going out with Adrian, and now Dal had to go and say something like that?

Dal nudged him when a mechanic approached. It wasn't Ricky, his usual guy, but some ripped, tan unknown person heading their way. Chase looked up into the bluest eyes he had ever seen. The man was about the same height as Dal, maybe an inch or so shorter, and gorgeous, even with the grease smudges on his forehead and left cheek.

"I'm Kyler, and I'm assuming, from the way the other guys talk, you," the big guy rumbled, gesturing to Chase, "are Manny, the owner of the sweet Sabre I worked on today." The way he spoke was so matter-of-fact, Chase didn't even think to correct his name error.

"Actually, this is Chase Manning, and yes, the blue one is his," Dal explained.

Chase looked between the two men before his brain managed to kick in gear. "I'm Chase. How's my baby?" He knew his lilt was in full effect, but didn't care. The shop he used, Mickey's, always treated him right.

After a few minutes' discussion, Chase thanked Kyler and paid the bill. After slipping his helmet on, he mounted the bike, revving the engine a little.

Dal stepped up beside him, arms folded across his chest, waiting. Chase flipped his visor up and smiled.

"That's the grin that's been missing lately. Glad you've got your bike back. Now, do you have everything you need? All set?"

"Yes, Dad," Chase singsonged and winked.

"Don't tempt me, or you'll end up bent over my knee for the spanking you know you deserve," Dal countered and smirked.

Chase laughed as Dal took a good-natured swipe at him before heading back to his cruiser.

Once Dal got into his car, Chase shot out of the driveway, back onto the street, thrilled to be riding his bike again, even if it was still freakin' cold out. He knew he would look good tonight, and that was all that mattered.

"Eat your heart out, Rhys. I'm going to have a great evening… without you!" Chase yelled into the roar of his bike and the wind around him.

chapter eight

CHASE SAT in the waiting area at Louie's Downtown. It was five minutes until six, and Adrian was to meet him for their first date then. He was so nervous his left leg bounced, and he caught himself, more than once, toying with his lip ring. He still wasn't entirely certain this was his best idea. He liked Adrian, but the feeling he was doing something wrong, abandoning Rhys somehow, refused to leave him alone.

He had taken his time getting ready after work, having laid out his clothes that morning in preparation for their date. He hoped that the low-slung black dress slacks, coupled with his favorite hunter green silk button-down and a pair of his chunky boots made him look as good as he knew Adrian would.

Right at six o'clock the door opened and Adrian walked in, looking just as delicious as expected. Chase took a moment to peruse the lovely view. Adrian was decked out in a pair of dress jeans that showed off his form beautifully, along with a teal cashmere turtleneck and long frock coat. It made him want to throw off Adrian's coat and run his hands over the sweater and feel the muscles underneath.

Chase beamed at Adrian. "Hi." Chase signed. "You look wonderful."

"Thank you, Chase," Adrian signed and said. Chase was entranced for a moment by the light flush that spread across Adrian's face.

After letting the hostess know they were both there and ready, she led them to a small table. She handed them menus and left after telling them their server would be Carrie.

"This is nice," Adrian said, gesturing around the restaurant. "You come here a lot?"

"No. I had never been here until my best friend, Jamie, got engaged. They're going to cater his reception," Chase explained, his mouth already watering so much at the thought of scallops he didn't need to look at the menu.

A moment later, their server, Carrie, filled their water glasses, set a basket of bread down between them, and took their order. Chase was fascinated with how Adrian used his hands while talking, even with people that didn't understand sign.

"Wonderful." Adrian looked down for a moment before raising his eyes to meet Chase's again. "I was surprised you asked me to dinner."

"Why?" Chase asked. He had noticed Adrian's shock when he asked but had assumed it was a matter of him not being hit on by students often, ex or otherwise. Now he wasn't so sure. "You're handsome and smart and funny."

"I don't get too many invites from cute men, not after the grades have gone out." Adrian laughed, but his eyes retained a sense of sadness that made Chase wonder if maybe he had been used before, a concept he knew all too well from when he was younger. Not that twenty-six was exactly old, but some days it certainly felt it.

Chase started to comment, but two things distracted him. One event was welcome. The other inexplicable one was not! Carrie arrived and placed their salads in front of them. After refilling their drinks, she quietly stepped away.

Chase smiled at Adrian, then tasted his first bite of salad just as Rhys walked by, escorting some young guy to a table across from theirs. He nearly choked as he tried to force the bite down his throat.

Adrian put his fork down and reached for Chase's hand once he seemed to be breathing properly again. "You okay?"

"Yeah," he rasped, nodding to make sure Adrian understood him. "Just went down wrong."

After taking another drink, Chase glanced over to Rhys's table, grinding his teeth when he noticed they were holding hands. Turning back to his dinner date, Chase stabbed his salad a little more viciously than he intended, furious at himself for even caring about Rhys being there.

They didn't talk much during the meal, Chase finding it difficult to sign and eat at the same time. The other problem was that his gaze kept sliding to Rhys and his date, much against his wishes.

"So, tell me what you do when you're not flirting with teachers?" Adrian asked as they sat after finishing their meals.

"I run my own IT consulting firm, plus I help out at the Coiled Dragon."

"And when not doing that?" Adrian asked, a small smile making his handsome face enchanting.

Chase grinned back at him. "You have the sexiest voice," he commented and winked. Chase loved how Adrian both spoke and signed. It was sexy and helped him follow the conversation better. "Hanging out with friends, dancing, reading... you know, normal things. I—" He was distracted when the man with Rhys giggled. When he looked over, he saw the little tramp touching Rhys again. *God!* He wanted to rip the damn twink's hands off his. *No, I don't care what he does. He doesn't matter to me and he's not mine.* The little voice that asked why he kept looking then was not appreciated.

A gentle hand touching his startled Chase out of his irritated and irrational thoughts. "What is it?"

"Nothing. I'm sorry, Adrian."

"No, something about that couple over there bothers you. Do you know them?" The softly spoken question startled Chase. He hadn't realized he had been so noticeable in his distraction.

"I—Yes, but it doesn't matter."

Adrian continued to stare at him, as if waiting for something.

"Really, it doesn't matter. The big one over there," he explained, gesturing with one hand. "His name is Rhys. We were an almost, once upon a time." It was more complicated than that, of course, but he didn't really think Adrian needed or wanted the full history.

Adrian nodded. "Would you like to go for a little walk?"

Chase thought it over for a moment but agreed. Once he paid for their meal—he insisted even though Adrian attempted to swipe the bill—Adrian led him outside.

Chase slipped his coat on, then held Adrian's out for him, smoothing the lapels down before stepping back. Adrian took his hand and tugged him down the sidewalk. It was cold out, but he was happy to walk with Adrian. Well, until he started talking again.

"You are not truly over him, are you?" The way Adrian looked at Chase made him want to squirm, and not in a good way. His father gave him the same look when he knew Chase was going to lie.

"I—"

"It's okay, Chase. I've seen that look before. Hell, I've worn it myself." Adrian reached out and gently slid his fingers down Chase's cheek. "You were nervous and jittery before they arrived. Since then, it has gotten worse."

"Maybe, but I asked you out because I like you for who you are, not for who you're not, if that makes sense."

Adrian nodded. "I trust you, Chase."

Adrian moved slowly closer to him, tilted his head ever so slightly, and gently pressed his lips against Chase's. He froze for a moment, and then pushed into the kiss. Adrian kept it light, and after a few moments, Chase realized he felt nothing about the kiss. When Adrian pulled away, he was disappointed, but only with himself.

A small sigh escaped Adrian's lips and a sad smile spread across his face. "But I think you need a friend right now, more than a boyfriend."

Chase gaped at him. "Seriously?" He could feel his face heat, hating himself for being so easy to read.

"Very." Adrian's face suddenly split into a broad grin. "Do I still get that ride on your bike?"

Chase started laughing. "Come on! Friends get bike rides too," he signed and said. He took Adrian's hand again and tugged him back to his parked Sabre.

BY THE time Chase returned to his empty apartment, he was cold and couldn't seem to shake the feeling Adrian might be right about waiting longer before trying to date, or perhaps even trying to ask Rhys out, not that he thought the latter would help.

Chase dumped his bag, jacket, and helmet on the couch and headed to his bedroom, deciding a shower to thaw his freezing bones might be a good idea. Stripping quickly, he stepped into the bathroom and turned on the water to warm it up.

After stepping into the hot shower, Chase braced himself against the wall with his hands and let the water pound on his back, warming him as it loosened his tense muscles. His mind drifted to how Rhys had looked earlier that evening. How his powerful body had stretched the fine material of his chocolate button-down, his rich auburn hair tied back in the little ponytail Chase's fingers always itched to pull free. And, *God*, how he moved set Chase off. He almost prowled, with such power and grace he was certain there were large cats jealous of his sensuous movements and innate power.

He grabbed the body wash and lathered up his chest and abs, trying to ignore the fact his cock had taken an interest in his musings. As he continued to wash, his mind again focused on Rhys, but this time on their one night together. To how delicious Rhys's skin had tasted and felt beneath his teeth and tongue. The sounds the man had made as he filled him again and again.

Before he realized what he was doing, he'd wrapped his right hand tightly around his erection. Giving up on doing otherwise, Chase poured a little conditioner into his hand and took long strokes from base to crown, giving a slight squeeze and twist to the head. Continuing to pleasure himself, Chase let his desires free.

Picking up speed with each stroke, Chase leaned against the wall, widening his stance. He tweaked one nipple, then the other, pinching and rolling, dragging more groans out of himself. Eventually he cupped his sac, tugging and squeezing the way he liked, both adding to the pleasure and keeping him on the edge of bliss.

Pulling harder and faster, Chase pictured Rhys's lips wrapped around his throbbing cock—the heat and wetness of the shower became the inside of Rhys's mouth. At the last moment, Chase dropped his hand to massage and tease his opening, pressing in just as his orgasm hit, the pleasure overwhelming him as wave after wave of thick cream spurted into the running water. Chase didn't stop stroking himself until every drop was out and his skin felt too sensitive to continue.

Not wanting reality to invade his perfect high, Chase quickly rinsed and dried off with his eyes closed, attempting to keep the image of Rhys, blissed out and covered in his own come, clear in his mind. Chase climbed into bed, wrapped himself around one of the large pillows, and settled on the thought of how warm and content Rhys had looked as he drifted off to sleep.

THE NEXT morning, Chase got up early, knowing James, Dale, and Vaughn would arrive soon for breakfast. He was both glad and disappointed Simon wouldn't be there, but he figured he would not have to listen to any "told you sos" about picking his own date from the others. But then, his choice of dates had bombed too, but for a very different reason than Si's choices always did.

His mind flashed back to the night before, when Adrian had kissed him. The man had soft, gentle lips. Lips that under normal conditions he would have loved to nibble and kiss until they were swollen and red, but the only lips his mind seemed to conjure when he thought of passion and heat were Rhys's. Of course, that brought to mind his shower from the night before.

Annoyed at the warmth spreading throughout his body, Chase willed his rapidly hardening cock to lie down and behave. When that didn't work too well, he reminded himself of the guy on Rhys's arm at the restaurant, hoping to squash the longing he still felt.

Trying, again, to push such thoughts away, Chase started pulling out the ingredients for his cinnamon vanilla french toast, as per the text requests he'd awakened to find that morning. He was just pulling out the bacon and juice when he heard the first set of rat-a-tat-tats on his front door. He realized he was wearing only a pair of threadbare jeans as he opened his door.

"Oh, man candy and breakfast? My fave," Vaughn teased. "Still think you need to get one of these pierced," he continued with a smirk and reached out to quickly pinch one of Chase's nipples before ducking past him and fleeing into the apartment.

Chase hissed at the touch—they were both still a little sensitive from how rough he'd been on them the night before. "Hey, those are not for you to play with," Chase growled back, playfully chasing Vaughn through the apartment.

"Now, now, boys. Play nice." Dale followed them inside and looked around, then quirked a brow at Chase. "Where's James? We are *never* here first."

"Seems you are today. Jamie texted me earlier, so I know he will be here soon. Now, why don't one of you go set the table while I get the bacon cooking and finish the toast," Chase instructed. He said the same thing every time they came over to eat.

After a moment, Chase heard the stereo go on in the living room. Before long, the sounds of "Madness" by Muse surrounded him, and he found he was dancing while cooking.

By the time he was plating their food, James arrived. They all sat down and started eating immediately.

"So, how was the date last night?" Dale asked.

Chase frowned, not sure he wanted to discuss his problem with them, even if they were his best friends.

"Oh no, that bad?" Vaughn leaned over, giving him a half hug. "Was the guy not nice to you or something?"

"No, nothing like that. Adrian is really very sweet. He's smart, funny, and patient. He didn't even tease when I messed up some of my signs," Chase added with a tiny smile. "He's great, but... not for me?"

James set his fork down before speaking. "What went wrong, then, Chase? You were so excited about this one. It's not still Rhys, is it?"

He winced at the sound of Rhys's name. Chase could tell they all caught it too. "The damn man had the audacity to show up at Louie's with anoth—with some boy."

The three other men looked at each other, and if he didn't know better, he would swear Dale smirked.

"Thought you said you were over what happened and he hadn't hurt you. You want to add anything to your story?" Jamie added, picking his fork back up and taking another bite of french toast.

Chase's gaze snapped up to meet James's. "I told you before he didn't hurt me, but even now that I know he lied about what he thinks of me and my appearance, it wouldn't work. And don't any of you," he added quickly, pointedly staring at each man in turn, "think you know better than me on this one."

"We would never presume such a thing," Dale said, his tone so serious Chase knew he was being mocked. Dale was never that serious, ever!

"Humph! I'm not playing these games with you three. Now, eat up. We need to get to the shop for our final fitting," Chase crooned, grinning at James.

"Yeah," James sighed, looking off into the distance with the same dopey, love-struck look Chase had seen for months whenever his wedding was mentioned.

After they'd eaten and cleaned up, they headed out as a group to the tux shop. Even though Chase and James had tuxedos, they were getting all new clothes so everyone coordinated perfectly.

chapter nine

CHASE PULLED up as close as possible to the front of the Onyx Rose B&B, the site where the rehearsal dinner and wedding reception were being held, barely taking in the beautiful setting. He had been here before, of course, seeing as it was the first in a chain of GLBTQ hotels Carrington Enterprises—Seth Burns specifically—designed and owned. If it weren't for the building before him, James and Seth would never have met, and there would be no pending nuptials.

A young man darted over, offering assistance. Chase smiled, thankful for the full service offered, even though it was set up as a B&B and not a traditional, stuffy hotel. "Can you grab me one of those big dolly things? I have a lot to transport inside and need to do so quickly."

In a matter of minutes, Chase—with Chad the valet's help—had the tuxes and other apparel for the wedding party, the programs, and a few early wedding presents loaded. Chase tossed the man his keys and headed inside to start delivering items.

Even though he lived in the area, as did much of the wedding party, they were all staying at the Onyx Rose. That evening, they would hold the rehearsal dinner, and tomorrow evening, the wedding itself—well, the public wedding. The legal one would be in Iowa in the morning.

An hour later, Chase stopped in front of Rhys and Dal's room to drop off their things, and froze. Why he couldn't just forget about the damn man, he did not know. However, showing up at Rhys's hotel door was not on Chase's list of happy things to do. Nope, Rhys was definitely not on his bucket list. Taking a deep breath, Chase raised his fist and gave a light knock, hoping no one would be there… or maybe just Dal. Dal he could handle just fine, but he so didn't want to see—

Before he could continue that thought, the door opened. The sight before him nearly brought Chase to his knees. Rhys was in a pair of jeans that hung low on his tapered hips. They highlighted his thick, muscular thighs. Chase wasn't entirely sure how they even stayed up with how low they sat. That was also the only thing he wore—well, other than the towel he was using to dry his hair.

"Yeah?" Rhys asked. He stopped, and his eyes widened as he stared at Chase.

It took Chase a moment to form words that weren't likely to get him in trouble. "Uh, um, Rhys? I, I have yours and Dal's stuff. I'm just, um—"

"Calm down, Chase. You know it doesn't bother me to have you here, so take a deep breath, please."

Chase went from flustered to irritated in a half second flat. How dare the man tease him like that? "I don't need you to help me breathe, thank you very much. I was trying to say I have your tuxedos and… things. Would you mind?" he snapped, pointing to the dolly where both men's items hung.

Rhys's gaze followed Chase's slender hand as he gestured but then snapped back to Chase's face again. "No, I don't mind. Here, let me help you," Rhys continued, his voice low and husky. He stepped into Chase's space, brushing his massive, naked chest against Chase's outstretched arm as he reached around to grab the two garment bags.

Chase couldn't stifle the gasp fast enough as the heat shot through him at the touch, his mind flashing again to their one night together. As Rhys drew back, his free hand gently settled on Chase's shoulder, his thumb barely grazing Chase's throat.

"Thank you for picking everything up, Chase." Rhys caressed up and down Chase's skin with his thumb, leaving goose bumps in its wake.

"No, no problem," Chase squeaked. He could feel the warmth spread across his face, but he couldn't manage to tear himself away from Rhys's touch or gaze. "I should go," he added, though he made no move to leave.

Rhys grunted, though he didn't notice or care if it was in agreement or not. Chase wanted to step into the man before him and devour him whole, but the memory of Garrett's name on his lips and the twink on Rhys's arm held him back.

Chase cleared his throat and finally looked away. "Well, I'll catch you later. Please tell Dal hi for me. He owes me a drink and a dance."

The small smile that turned up Rhys's lips made his heart hurt. "I'll let him know. I look forward to seeing you later." With that said, he broke physical contact, letting Chase breathe finally.

Once the door was shut, Chase made it partway down the hall before he stopped and leaned back against the wall, and then closed his eyes. He had no idea what to do about his attraction to Rhys. One portion of him wanted to say screw it and go for a real relationship with the gentle giant, but the rest of him knew how much the man could hurt him if his assumptions about Rhys were correct. Right then he wished he had a cold drink, a comfy pile of cushions to flop down in, and James to talk to, but he couldn't burden his best friend with all his drama—not the night before his wedding! Maybe not ever.

Chase was pulled out of his musings when someone touched his shoulder lightly. "Chase? Are you all right?"

Startled, Chase righted himself and drew away from the wall. He looked up, surprised to see Dal peering down at him. "Yeah, fine," he mumbled as he smoothed his hands down his thighs.

"You sure? You jumped a foot in the air, and seriously, you didn't hear me coming down the hall?"

"I'm just a little worn out. There's a lot that goes into a wedding, ya know," Chase teased, though it sounded a little flat to him. "Anywhozit, Rhys has your tux."

"You talked to Rhys?" Dal asked, his face lighting up like a little kid's. Chase hated that look! Meant Dal was still hopeful Chase and Rhys would get together, permanent like—an idea that held both interest and fear for him.

"Yeah," he mumbled, looking down at his feet. Suddenly he snapped up his head and grinned. "So... you bringing anyone special to the wedding? Some cute girl? Or maybe some delish guy?" he asked as he waggled his eyebrows.

Dal laughed, the deep rumbling sound making Chase smile even wider. "Um, no. I'm not bringing a date."

"Aw, why not? I heard you met someone recently. Not ready to show him or her off yet?"

The flush that swept over Dal's face delighted Chase beyond reason. He was glad the topic had changed. Besides, he wanted his friend happy, and that flush said the mystery someone was definitely interesting to one Dal Sayer. "I, um, no, it's not like that. We've only spoken a couple of times, and we haven't even gone out yet."

"Have you even asked?"

If it were possible, Dal turned a deeper share of red—even his ears and throat pinked up. "No, he's so cute and sexy and, I don't know. I mean, he doesn't seem to like cops much. I swear he flirted a little, but...."

"But you're scared?"

Dal nodded, not quite meeting Chase's eyes. "Rhys offered to do a background check on him, but I said no."

"Are you tattling on me again, Dal?" Rhys's voice slid up Chase's spine, causing him to shiver before he could control it. Rhys was standing behind him. The man had sneaked up on them as they talked, unnoticed by him and unannounced by Dal.

"Hey, it's my job, right?" The sudden grin on Dal's face was precious.

"Depends on what and to whom," Rhys quipped, gently shoving Dal's shoulder.

"Boys, behave," Chase snapped, the grin on his face belying the harshness of his words. "Don't make me separate you two."

Both men looked down at Chase, then at each other before chuckling loudly. "You and whose army, little man?" Rhys said, his voice deep, sensual.

"I don't need an army to control the likes of you, big man," Chase replied in the same tone, head tilted slightly to the right. His voice dropped again as he continued, "And you will be good, won't you, Sayer?"

Chase watched in delight as Rhys swallowed hard, his Adam's apple bobbing so hard it drew his eyes for a moment. He nodded, shifting his weight from one foot to the other. "For you, I would," he whispered so softly Chase almost didn't hear him.

They stood frozen, gazing into each other's eyes for a moment before Chase managed to tear his gaze away.

"We're not doing this, Rhys," Chase mumbled before he turned on his heel, grabbed the dolly, and left both men standing in the hall, whispering behind him. He couldn't figure out why he'd baited Rhys, but he needed to get it under control before he did something truly insane. No matter what James or Adrian or even Dal said, Rhys was dangerous to his heart. He wasn't ready to risk everything for a man who already had two strikes against him in the partner column. Why no one else could figure out they were better off not together, he did not know.

He was certain—well, mostly, maybe—if he told James everything, he would at least be on Chase's side. But for whatever reason, Chase had been unable to reveal what had happened that night.... That one perfect night—until the end, that was.

FLITTING BETWEEN tables, Chase checked the settings and place cards, making sure everything was exactly as it should be before he met with the others for the wedding rehearsal. He wanted everything perfect for James and Seth. Satisfied that everything met with his approval, Chase turned and came face to face with Rhys. The wedding and reception were going to be the end of him, he was certain, as Rhys seemed determined to flirt, follow, and watch him at every turn.

"You needing something, Rhys?" Chase asked, annoyed when he heard how raspy he sounded. It was bad enough he couldn't get the man out of his fantasies, but even his voice was betraying him now!

"Oh, I need something all right, but for now, I just wanted to see if you wanted any help." Chase lifted his eyebrow as he stared at Rhys, making him squirm. "I, oh, never mind."

Chase released a sigh and deflated some. He knew Rhys liked him, but being rude over an offer of help was beyond petty, something he was ashamed to admit to being a lot lately.

"No, I'm done, but thank you, Rhys."

The smile he got in return was breathtaking, and his heart melted a little more. He knew he was losing the battle with his heart and loins, but he wasn't ready to give in. Not yet. Hearing Rhys call out his ex's name still rang through his mind.

"Would you like a ride to the rehearsal?" Rhys asked, his voice deeper than before.

"The church is just down the road, ya know," Chase chirped. The tone Rhys used shot straight to his cock. He was half-hard and desperately hoping Rhys wouldn't notice.

Rhys shrugged his broad shoulders, smiling softly. "And?"

Chase bit his bottom lip, thinking. He wanted to say yes, to sit behind the delicious man in front of him, his groin pressed to Rhys's lower back with the deep rumble and vibrations of the bike beneath them.

"I'll be good, Chase. I promise."

Chase let out a soft groan. *Oh, you're that, all right! Damn you!* "Fine. But we need to hurry. I can't be late." He knew he was making excuses to himself, but an offer of free touching with a nonsexual justification? Yeah, he was so there!

HOW THE hell did I end up here? Chase took another sip of his fourth—or was it his fifth, not counting the shots somewhere in between—mojito as he looked around the club. The same club where he'd met Rhys the first time. After the rehearsal and dinner, a group of guys had decided they needed to hit the clubs—ignoring the fact that neither James nor Seth went along with them. His gaze again caught on Rhys as he danced with a group of friends. *Why does he have to be so gorgeous and addictive? Ugh!*

A strong hand settled on his shoulder, and a deep voice in his ear startled him out of his thoughts. "Come dance with us, Chase," Dal rumbled. "One dance won't kill ya, and I know you love to dance. Come on."

The plea and touch both excited and frustrated him. He wanted Rhys to be the one begging him, not Dal. *No, I don't. I do not want Rhys, dammit!* The little voice in his head mocking him with *"I think the gentleman doth protest too much"* was not helping. Deciding *what the hell*, he stood, letting Dal drag him onto the dance floor.

As usual, as soon as Chase hit the dance floor, dancing, writhing bodies surrounded him. He smiled as Dal grabbed Chase's hips and pulled him closer. "Come on, lose the shirt, Chase!" Dal called as he grabbed the hem of Chase's tight indigo T-shirt and pulled it up over his head.

70

Chase grabbed it back, tucked one corner of it into one of the pockets of his tight jeans, and put his hands on Dal's wide shoulders.

As they ground against each other, dancing, Chase looked up at Dal, almost able to pretend he was Rhys. As soon as the thought crossed his mind, he winced, hating himself for such a thought. He would never use someone like that, especially not someone as sweet and loving as Dal.

Dal suddenly spun him around, pulling him so his back pressed to Dal's front. He could feel a rather impressive bulge against his lower back. Warm breath tickled across his ear and cheek as Dal chuckled next to his ear. "You are such a cock tease, Chase," he moaned, rubbing against Chase's ass hard.

"Sorry," he breathed. "I-I don't mean to be."

"Oh, I know." Dal's hands moved up Chase's abs to his chest, pinching his nipples and twisting them a little as he continued to murmur in Chase's ear. "I'm not the Sayer you want, but damn, you're hot enough to make me forget who we each actually want right now."

Chase laughed at him. "You should have brought your cutie with you, Dal. We could have danced together." He punctuated his words by wrapping his arms around Dal's neck behind him, continuing to rub against him. He knew they were both being stupid, but he was too drunk to care, especially when he could see Rhys grinding on some skanky rent boy across the dance floor.

They continued dancing and teasing one another for two more songs. When Dal whirled him around to face him again, Chase had a sudden flash of worry, fear that Dal might try to take things further—an idea both intriguing and horrid. It would ruin so much for four men if that ever happened. Plus, Dal wasn't what his body or heart wanted.

The unexpected hands on his hips from behind didn't worry him, not in a club like this, but the way Dal's eyes went wide and he suddenly stepped back did. Before he could see who it was, Chase felt more than heard a voice he would recognize anywhere. "What the hell are you doing practically having sex in the middle of the dance floor with my brother, Chase?"

He whimpered as Rhys pushed his impressive erection against his ass, already so horny he was about to climb Rhys right then and ride him—damn the consequences and his preferences. He wanted Rhys and was just drunk enough to dismiss the warnings going off in his head.

Without thinking about it, he pulled Rhys down and slanted his mouth over Rhys's. Rhys instantly opened for the violent assault, tangling his tongue with Chase's as soon as he licked inside Rhys's mouth. Chase groaned again, pushing and tugging at Rhys, continuing the punishing kiss as he wrapped himself around Rhys, making him support his weight.

Rhys reached down and grabbed his ass, lifting him off his feet. Chase immediately wrapped his legs around Rhys, never breaking the kiss. When his need for air finally made him pull back, Rhys chased his lips even as they both panted.

"Chase, please," Rhys begged. "You haveta take me home with you!"

Cutting off any further words, Chase delved back into the kiss, thrusting against Rhys's tight abs. "Cab?" he panted, pulling back only long enough to bark the word before taking Rhys's lips again.

He felt Rhys moving, he hoped toward the door. When he was finally set on the floor again, Dal was standing there, holding the door open, smiling at him. Maybe smirking would have been a better description. "I grabbed you a taxi already. Go on, you two," he added with a wink.

Refusing to second-guess anything right then, Chase yanked his shirt back on, grabbed Rhys's hand, and dragged him out of the club and to the waiting cab. As soon as the door closed behind them, he gave the driver the address of the Onyx Rose.

He made Rhys stay on his side of the car, not wanting to deal with a cabbie putting up a fuss if they kept making out as they had been. He concentrated on his shoes and his breathing to prevent himself from pouncing on Rhys and *damn the consequences*!

chapter ten

AS RHYS dipped in for another kiss, Chase stretched up to meet him in a devouring, soul-searing crashing of lips. Before Chase knew what was happening, Rhys pushed him against the door and lifted him enough that Chase's feet no longer touched anything. The power and strength Rhys displayed shot straight to his cock, making him hungrier for the not-so-gentle giant now ravaging him.

Chase slid his hands up and down Rhys's sides before moving slowly to unbutton his dress shirt. Rhys was busy holding and kneading his backside as he held him tighter. Never breaking the kiss, he pulled at the bottom of the shirt to untuck it before he finished unbuttoning it. Once it was out of the way, Chase ran his fingers along Rhys's firm pecs, reveling in the strength he found. When he rubbed, then pinched one nipple, Rhys reared back. He groaned and shivered against Chase, his eyes closed tight as he panted hard.

"Chase, please," Rhys ground out.

"Please what, Rhys? Please stop? Please more? What do you want, boy?"

"Not. A. Boy," Rhys countered, grinding his swollen member against Chase through their clothes.

Chase vibrated, nearly in pain at the thought of being inside Rhys again. "Bed, now!"

Rhys backed up enough to allow Chase to slide down his body before leaning over to continue the ravaging kiss, moving to nip at Chase's jaw.

It took Chase only a moment to realize he was being manhandled over to one of two huge king-sized beds in the middle of the room. He allowed the maneuvering but stopped when he felt the bed against the back of his legs. He teased around the edge of Rhys's pants before unbuttoning them with quick, controlled motions. He slid down the zipper and tugged them off Rhys's hips, to pool at their feet.

Chase again took one nipple, this time with his mouth, tracing around the tight bud with the tip of his tongue before sucking it into his mouth and nibbling on it. The growl Rhys released was very satisfying and only served to egg him on more. He pinched and tugged on the other one as he kept the suction and nibbling up on the first, determined to reduce Rhys to a begging, trembling mass of sexy man.

"God," Rhys yelled when Chase's other hand slid around to his ass, digging his fingers into the meaty flesh there.

"No, you don't call his name. You only call mine."

"Huh?" Rhys sounded confused, but Chase didn't care.

"You call my name," Chase again demanded. He punctuated the order by pinching and twisting harder on the nipple between his fingers. "Say my name, Rhys."

"Chase!"

Please, please, please have thought ahead, Chase begged mentally. He'd not intended to take Rhys to bed again, at least not yet, so he wasn't as prepared as he should have been.

He squeezed and rubbed Rhys's length, enjoying the tremble and the mewling noises coming from him. "Supplies, in my bag," Rhys barely managed to gasp out, flailing toward a black duffel beside them.

Chase pointed at the bag, one eyebrow quirked. Rhys immediately dropped into a squat, pulled the bag over, and rummaged in the side, a triumphant look on his face as he presented the items to Chase.

He tugged Rhys back to standing before pushing him until he sat on the edge of the bed. Chase prowled closer, taking his fill of how decadent Rhys looked as he kicked off his shoes and slacks.

The moment he was in range, Rhys started working on Chase's buttons. One of Chase's hands snapped out, snagging Rhys's wrist to stop him; the other went to his hair, tugging Rhys's head back sharply to meet his eyes. "No. You watch. You don't touch without permission."

Chase watched in satisfaction as Rhys swallowed but nodded, dropping his hands. Chase took a step back and ran his hands over his tight, indigo silk-and-spandex T-shirt-clad chest, taking time to rub his nipples as Rhys trembled, hands gripping the edge of the bed hard. The growl and moan he heard from the other man had him so excited, he almost skipped the teasing. Almost. After a few moments, Chase began to slowly inch the shirt up his lithe body, deliberately torturing the delicious man before him.

Once the shirt was off and set aside, Chase toed off his shoes and socks before moving to stand between Rhys's thighs. Rhys moved forward as if in a trance, trembling as he panted.

Chase started to speak, but the sudden pinch and pull of his belt silenced him. When Rhys's fingers slipped just under the waistband of the trousers, Chase gasped and jutted his hips out more, sucking in his tight abs to make it easier for Rhys to unbutton and unzip.

The dark silk boxers under Chase's pants helped them shift down faster so he could step out of them. Rhys took his time looking up and down Chase's body, swallowing hard when his gaze again zeroed in on Chase's package, something the boxers did nothing to hide.

Rhys started to push down those boxers when Chase stopped him. "No, not yet, Rhys. Up," Chase demanded, tugging Rhys back to standing. Once up, Chase quickly divested Rhys of the last of his clothing, taking in the size and breadth of the man before him.

Before he could second-guess himself, Chase dropped to his knees, rubbing his face against Rhys's swollen cock, chuckling lightly at the gasps and twitches his touch elicited. Chase took a deep breath, reveling in the deep, musky scent that enveloped him. Running his hands up and down Rhys's thighs, Chase nuzzled the base of the gorgeous cock before him, his mouth watering.

Taking pity on Rhys, Chase nudged him. "Sit, big guy. I don't want you falling on me."

Rhys moved faster than he would have believed possible, yet was still somehow graceful. Once he was seated, Chase ran one finger up the underside, tracing the vein until he got to the head. Using his thumb, he spread the viscous fluid weeping there around the soft, silky skin. He teased and toyed with the foreskin a moment, enjoying the sounds the light touches drew out of Rhys.

Chase was so focused on the member before him, he was startled when Rhys suddenly threaded his hands through Chase's hair, gripping and yanking him forward a little. He couldn't help the moan that slipped out: while he preferred to be in charge, he did love the power and strength a partner like Rhys could bring to the bed.

"You may tug or touch, but don't you dare pull my hair out. It's also not a handle," Chase said, batting his eyes and deliberately jerking his head away to make Rhys pull his hair again.

"Fine, but please, Chase... stop teasing."

The whimper that came out of Rhys when Chase finally wrapped his lips around the crown made him chuckle. He loved having the power to reduce a man to a shivering mass of desire, though with Rhys it was somehow different than with anyone he'd been with before. A feeling he staunchly ignored as he set a fast pace, sucking and flicking his tongue around Rhys's cock as he hummed. He massaged Rhys's balls as he continued to devour his dick, loving the little noises and not so little thrusts. Drawing up to focus on the crown alone, he pulled down on Rhys's sack, a little harder and longer each time.

"Oh God! Please, Chase.... Oh, fuck me! Gonna... gonna, ohhh...." Rhys bellowed as he suddenly shot down Chase's throat. Chase swallowed greedily, making sure not to miss a drop. He continued to lick and tug until Rhys was writhing and whimpering again.

Chase considered pulling down his boxers and getting off right then, but decided he wasn't done with Rhys, whether the big guy knew it or not. Slowly he climbed up onto the bed, dragging Rhys with him.

Letting Rhys have enough time to calm his breathing some, Chase continued to pet and caress him the entire time. When he thought Rhys was composed enough, he leaned in and nibbled Rhys's bottom lip lightly. "Ya know." Rubbing his leaking cock against Rhys's grooved abs, Chase murmured against his lips, "I still have a problem here, and only your pretty little ass will do, Rhys. I'm gonna fill you up, then *fill* you up!"

GASPING AWAKE, he tried to turn over. Chase realized there was a heavy furnace sprawled across his lower back and shoulders. It took him another moment to dredge through his memories from the night before.... *Rhys? O M G!*

Before he could decide what to do or how he felt about what he'd done—*again!*—he was rolled and pulled back against Rhys. He could feel how hard Rhys was as he ground against Chase and murmured against his ear, "G'morning."

Chase closed his eyes as Rhys's mouth traveled down his throat, nipping, sucking, and kissing before finally returning to his ear, where he gently bit down on the fleshy bit. Without thinking, he pushed back against Rhys and moaned. "Morning."

He moaned again as Rhys slid his hand down his chest and began rubbing circles across his abs, lower with each circling but never quite reaching his now eager shaft. "I love the little noises you make. So sexy."

"Damn," Chase groaned when Rhys finally wrapped his huge hand around his throbbing cock. Struggling to regain some kind of control, Chase cleared his throat. "Rhys, we shouldn't—"

"Yes, Chase, we should." Rhys kept up his dual assault on Chase, stroking him just the way he liked while continuing to nip and nuzzle at his neck and ear. "God, I want you. Please don't run again," he begged, his voice so deep Chase felt more than heard him.

Chase whimpered as what Rhys was doing mixed with his own desire for the man who held him. The clench of want in his gut had him nearly begging, demanding some form of satisfaction from his dream man. Though he knew this was real—*oh God was it ever*—he didn't want to think about later, when the "real world" would again intrude, and he would have to face what he had done and what was probably going to happen now.

He suddenly found himself flat on his back and the covers ripped off their bodies. Rhys moved so fast, it startled Chase, but before he could protest the new position, Rhys swallowed his cock to the root. Rhys set a fast pace as he bobbed up and down, the slurping sounds driving Chase mad with want.

Pulling off with a *pop*, Rhys looked up into Chase's eyes. "Damn, baby, you taste so good," he growled, before once again devouring Chase whole.

Chase grasped the sheets next to him, his other hand traveled downward to settle under the heavy fall of Rhys auburn hair, alternately massaging the base of his skull and playing with the hair at the nape of his neck.

"Rhys, *oh God!* I'm…. Can't…. Please…." Chase begged, thrusting his hips to plunge deeper into Rhys's mouth even as he tried to call out a warning.

Instead of backing off, Rhys dropped a hand to Chase's balls, kneading with gentle tugs added as he hollowed his cheeks with mind-numbing suction. Keening his pleasure, Chase emptied down Rhys's throat, shaking and arching off the bed. Never letting go of Rhys's hair as he lost track of time, place, and reason, his reality whited out.

After a while, though he had no idea how long it was, the world came back into focus, and Rhys leaned over him saying his name repeatedly. "Chase? Cariadon?"

The look on Rhys's face baffled him. "Rhys?"

"Oh, thank God! You had me worried, baby."

Chase looked down, confused.

Rhys cradled his head with large, strong hands, lifting his face until their eyes met again. "Chase, baby, you passed out on me or something. Are you okay now?"

The gentleness and compassion in Rhys's voice and motions caused a lump to form in his throat. Chase nodded, not certain his voice would work right then.

"What, what did you just call me?" At Rhys's blank look, he explained, "You said something other than 'Chase.'"

Rhys looked confused, but then his eyes widened. "Um, nu, nothing."

"Rhys!"

"*Cariadon.* It means 'love' or 'dear one' in Welsh," he mumbled.

Chase quickly gazed around the room, not ready to deal with what Rhys was saying, and his gaze landed on the alarm clock on the nightstand behind Rhys and froze. "Oh my God! Please tell me that's not the time."

"Huh?" Rhys looked over his shoulder then back at Chase. "Uh, yeah. I think that's about right. Why?"

"Why?" Did the man seriously just ask him that? "Oh, I don't know. Maybe because I should be downstairs in like five minutes to meet James

78

and Seth. I'm one of the witnesses for their legal wedding this morning. You know they're flying to Iowa for that one, and then this evening they do the public one. Mel and I, as the best men, are going with them. Damn, damn dammit! I gotta shower and get dressed and get down there fast. Ugh! I've got to get back to my room first," Chase snapped, glowering at Rhys. He knew it wasn't Rhys's fault, but he hated being late, and today was the wrong day to fall behind.

Before Rhys could respond, Chase was up, throwing his clothes from the night before back on and practically flying out the door, leaving a confused and frustrated Rhys in his wake.

RHYS STOOD by the large bed he and Chase had shared only moments before, wondering if he should be worried Chase was using the wedding as an excuse or if the smaller man was right, and he really was running late for his best friend's legal wedding before the public wedding. Before he could get too maudlin, his phone rang.

He scooped up his jeans, pulling out his cell to check the display.

"Mark? What's up this morning," he asked, forcing his voice to be more cheerful than he felt.

"Nothing good, man. There's been another suicide, but this time our cop friends think there might be something hinky—their word—about the scene. Think you can come in for a little bit?"

"Yeah," he mumbled. He figured his time would be better spent focusing on solving who was killing gay guys in town than sitting around the B&B mooning over Chase, especially if their department contacts were asking for help now. "But I have to be back in time for the ceremony. I mean, I am part of the wedding party and all."

"That shouldn't be a problem, man. Just want to get a few things started. You know the drill."

"I do. All right, be there in a bit." Rhys hung up before moving to take a shower and get dressed for work.

As he set out twenty minutes later, it suddenly dawned on him that Dal had never come back to their room. Bemused, he thought back to how Dal had acted with Chase the night before and wondered if he'd deliberately set out to make him jealous and get him to stake a claim on

Chase, or if he hadn't come back because he'd found someone else to go home with. The latter idea bothered him as much as the former, but he pushed it to the back of his mind, deciding he could always ask later.

When he got to his bike out front, he smiled at what was on the seat: a single white rose tied with a ribbon and a short note.

Forgive my abrupt leaving, Rhys, but I had to go. Maybe we could discuss whatever this is between us soon?
C

Grinning despite what he was leaving to deal with, he felt lighter than he had in ages. A sense of hope for the future took hold for the first time in years. He tucked the rose and note in his jacket, then headed to the office. *Wonder how you save a flower?*

chapter eleven

THE ROOM was overflowing with calla lilies, rose petals and buds, ribbon, and the finest linen, all in crisp white, pale dusky blue, or soft silver, giving everything a light, romantic feel. The expansive room filled with soft notes wafting about as if in invitation to come, sit, and relax. To one side there was a huge dance floor, and to the other was the reception area, already heavily laden with the wedding cake, a fully stocked bar, and more tables than Chase had any interest in counting, though he knew the number and had personally helped to plan and set out the place cards.

The wedding party was still decked out in their matching classic gray cutaway-style tuxedos with dusky blue and silver diagonal-striped euro tie and waistcoat. Each man also wore a silver-wrapped and accented double Picasso calla lily boutonniere. James's had a tiny paintbrush worked into his, while Seth's held a miniature Celtic tree of life and griffin charms. Well, they had—for the wedding and during all the innumerable pictures, and for about the first thirty seconds of the reception. After that, all bets were off on who was still posh and who was relaxed and a little rumpled.

As the dinner and speeches wore on—Chase was certain he'd never heard so many toasts in his life—the dance floor opened up for partiers to enjoy. As Seth walked up to him, Chase wondered how long before the music and dancing would shift from elegant to fun and loud.

"Chase?" Seth extended his hand, a soft smile on his lips. "Would you do me the honor of a dance?"

"Me?" Chase squeaked.

"Traditionally, it's a mother's or father's dance, but as you're the only member of James's family…." he trailed off, his hazel eyes piercing.

"Really?"

"Well, now that he and I are married, he has Danni and me, but yes, you are his family, so please," Seth asked again, holding his hand out.

"I'd be honored, sir."

The two men took to the dance floor, smiling as they quietly tried to one-up the other. The crowd laughed and catcalled until the song was over, and Seth moved on to another dance partner.

Chase went back to the bar to get another drink. Tonight, though, he was more careful about alcohol consumption, not ready to deal with the events of the previous night, or the morning for that matter. The shoulder bump startled him just before he managed his first sip of the Jack and Coke, hold the Jack.

"Come here often?" a deep, rumbling voice teased.

"Oh God," Chase groaned. "That has to be the lamest pickup line. Ever." Chase turned and took in the man before him. Dal, dressed to the nines in his formal wear, was breathtaking. Almost as amazing as his wayward brother.

"No, I've heard worse. Trust me."

Chase smirked.

"Sad but true. So, why're you over here instead of out there showing off?"

He shrugged. "Just needed a drink before I return to the happy couple." Chase looked to where his best friend and his new husband were sitting, Seth having escaped the dance floor again. "Jamie looks so good," he added softly. He was happy for his BFF yet jealous of him at the same time.

"Yeah, he does. They both do."

Mel, Seth's best man and lawyer friend, appeared at their side, all flushed grins and joy. "Chase, there you are. You ready?"

"Yep. Give me just a minute and I'll begin. 'Kay?"

Mel nodded, turned, and headed back over to where his beautiful wife, Britt, stood. Dal raised his brow pointedly at Chase. "Begin what?"

"You'll see," Chase replied, barely able to get the words out past a sudden fit of giggles at the look on Dal's face.

"Should I be worried or supportive of whatever it is you two are up to?"

"Supportive, of course." Chase looked around the room, his gaze snagging on Rhys. What caught his eye was Rhys focused on him. Well, more the scowl fixed on his handsome face. Chase never had been able to figure out the man's mood swings; now was no different.

Dal cleared his throat, drawing his attention away from Rhys and the memories of their shared time together.

"Huh?"

"Chase, what are you and Mel up to, and what's so fascinating over there?"

"Oh, uh, nothing. I mean nothing's fascinating. As for what we're up to.... You wanna help?" Chase asked, batting his eyes as he looked up at Dal, his head cocked slightly.

The groan Dal let out only made Chase's smile bigger. "Why do I have a feeling I'm going to regret this?"

"No, no, no. I promise, this is a good thing. Now, come here and be my muscle," Chase explained, wrapping one hand around Dal's biceps and tugging. "Please?"

Dal grumbled but followed along, continuing to ask what they were doing, a question Chase steadfastly ignored.

A few minutes later, things set to his exacting specifications, his laptop ready, Chase motioned to the band and then to Dal, who was across the room. The music came to a halt as a drop-down screen covered a large section of wall. After another moment, Chase spoke. "Today we are here to celebrate the beginning of a new life for James and Seth, both as newlywed husbands and as fathers to their precious little one, Danni. I hope you will forgive the interruption and take a few moments to share their joy, their happiness, and their lives."

Chase signaled to Dal and hit the Enter key. Moments later, the screen filled with a slide show of each man's life and family. It included James's grandparents and some of his friends, though Chase skipped his estranged family. As the show wore on, the pictures took on a more loving and sweet tone of the two men together. Gasps and applause immediately spread around the room, as did the occasional chuckle and *aww*.

Once the show was over and the lights turned up again, Chase noticed that James sat in Seth's lap, cuddled against his chest—both were smiling. Shortly afterward, the dancing resumed.

Minutes later, Chase stood near the edge of the dance floor, debating what he wanted to do, when a hand landed on his shoulder. When he turned, he was faced with a teary-eyed James. "That was wonderful, Chase." He paused, swallowed hard, and threw his arms around Chase's neck. "Thank you," he added, his voice cracking at the end.

"I'm so happy for you, Jamie! Now, go give that sexy man of yours a hug for me."

James tightened his arms for a moment before pulling back to look Chase over. "I will. I think I'll leave you for now, though. It looks like someone else wants your attention, dear," he murmured and smiled.

As James headed back to where Seth waited, Chase turned and was suddenly faced with Rhys. He stood tall, Rhys's strength seemingly captured and accentuated in the formal wear he wore.

"Yes, hun?" Chase asked and smiled. He debated between running away and throwing his arms around Rhys's neck and kissing him stupid.

A huge smile broke across Rhys's handsome, chiseled face as he took a single step. "Hello, Chase. Would you care to dance?"

Chase gulped hard, amazed as always by the beauty and size of the man before him. "I, um…."

Rhys took advantage of Chase's moment of indecision to move closer, their shoes nearly touching. "Chase?"

"Why?" Chase stared up into Rhys's iridescent green eyes, entranced yet terrified. He knew his strength to resist Rhys was at an end, but he still feared the pain he knew would come when Rhys left him. They all left in the end.

"Because…. Because, I have wanted to dance with you since the first time I saw you."

Chase scowled, snapping at Rhys, but Rhys held up his hand, placing his fingers against his lips, effectively derailing his thoughts. After a moment, Rhys continued. "I know I was stupid and ran you off the night we met. I have regretted that moment from about five seconds after the words came out of my mouth."

"It will only end in hurt feelings and pain, Rhys." Even Chase could hear the mingled sadness and lack of conviction in his words.

"I have no intention of giving up on you, Chase. Wrap your cute little self around that fact and take a chance on me. On us."

Chase looked around, hunting for a way to escape. Rhys had already stolen his heart and hurt him twice. No man ever got more than one screw-up…. Well, not until Rhys. When he realized everyone important to him seemed to be watching them, Chase shifted his feet, closing his eyes as he fought for strength. "I really don't think—"

"I know you don't," Rhys interrupted. His left hand slid up Chase's throat, a gentle caress Chase leaned into before he realized what he was doing. "But you're wrong, and I'm not going to give up on you. I will not harass you, but I intend to win your heart. No matter how long I have to wait for you to realize we are perfect for each other."

"You're going to what?" Chase barely got out, his voice nothing more than a whisper.

"Court you. Woo you. Whatever you want to call it. I know you care for me too, Chase. Please give in and allow us a real chance?" Rhys stepped back, extending his right hand.

Chase stared at the hand, calculating what his chances were of escaping Rhys, how much trouble he'd be in if he ran, and if his heart had any hope of surviving what he knew was going to happen. Quickly sweeping the room again, Chase swallowed hard and cleared his throat. He opened his mouth to accept, but nothing came out. He snapped it closed, mortified as he knew everyone stared at them. He finally managed a small nod, shivering hard when Rhys took his hand, gently pulling him toward the dance floor.

Rhys led, which was fine with Chase. While he liked to lead in the bedroom, he preferred the role he usually took out of it. After only a few steps, though, the area seemed to come to life, clapping and whistles barraging them. Chase cursed under his breath, at himself for accepting so publicly and at Rhys for being so open with his declaration of intent.

"I may never forgive you for this," Chase grumbled, though he made sure to keep a smile plastered on his face.

"I'll take my chances. You're worth it."

Against his wishes, he melted into Rhys's arms, reveling in his scent and strength as it wrapped around him, seeming to create a cocoon of warmth and hope around Chase.

AS THE guests lingered, watching James and Seth slide into the Rolls-Royce limo, Rhys pulled Chase back against his chest, arms wrapped around him tight. "Wave good-bye, sweetheart. I want one more dance before I have to head out."

Chase tensed in his arms for the first time in hours. "Head out? Where are you going?"

Rhys smiled, thankful Chase couldn't see him. "Unfortunately, the wicked don't rest. There are a few things I still need to tend to tonight at the office." He shrugged, hoping Chase wouldn't ask too much about the case. He did not want to tell him yet about the death. Not at a wedding.

"You need me on it?"

"No, not yet. Your part can wait until later, baby. Come dance and then walk me to my car?"

"Still not sure this is a good idea, but okay."

Pleased with Chase's acquiescence, Rhys pulled the slight man into his arms and moved with him as the music started again.

"Where did you learn to dance, by the way?"

"You didn't think I could dance?" Rhys asked, amused by the innocent question.

"No, yes. Not a lot of tough guys know how to ballroom dance, much less will admit to it. That's all I meant, hun."

"Relax, cariadon. You're so tense, it's like dancing with a board instead of the lithe man I know you to be." He hadn't meant to upset Chase, but sometimes maneuvering the minefield of what was and was not going to annoy Chase was beyond him. "And to answer you, Mom insisted Dal and I both learn to dance 'properly'." She'd been adamant he learn. At the time, he'd been angry with her. But now? Now Rhys was happy and made a mental note to thank her.

86

"Probably why you're so fluid and graceful when you move," Chase commented, seemingly unaware of the impact of his casual words. "Whatever the reason, I'm glad for it."

They continued dancing for the remainder of the song. When it ended, he pulled away, already missing Chase's body against his. "Thank you."

Chase looked up, meeting his eyes, and gave him such a sweet smile, he hated himself for needing to leave. "For what?"

Instead of answering, Rhys bent to brush his lips across Chase's. When Chase didn't pull back or complain, he decided to do it again, letting their lips press together. He increased the pressure, enjoying the slow movement as they danced together. Flicking his tongue out, he teased the seam of Chase's lips and the sexy little silver hoop there.

Chase parted his lips, but Rhys didn't deepen the kiss, happy to keep it light and building. Neither man noticed when the music started again, too focused on the simple pleasure of being together in that moment. When he finally pulled away, he looked down into the most beautiful eyes he had ever seen, pupils blown wide with desire. The soft sigh he heard brought him in for one last touch before he stood back and lifted Chase's right hand to his lips, kissing the underside of his wrist.

He ran the fingers of his other hand up Chase's throat, loving the shivers and soft sigh. "For giving me a chance. For the dance. For being you," he finally answered. "Please be safe tonight, okay?"

Chase nodded. "So, I'll see you at work Monday?"

Rhys closed his eyes, reminding himself he needed to spend more time with Chase, building trust between them, before inviting him back to his home. "Breakfast tomorrow?" he countered.

Chase looked at his watch and frowned. "Okay, but I'm so not cooking after everything today. Um," he continued, flicking the lip ring as he thought. "The coffee shop by your place at nine?"

"Sounds good, sweetheart. I really am sorry to go, but I have to. See you in the a.m." Rhys didn't wait for Chase to walk him out like he'd originally suggested, certain he wasn't strong enough to spend any more time with Chase without dragging him up to his room and begging to have his way with him again.

chapter twelve

CHASE STOOD out front of the shop he'd told Rhys to meet him at the night before, more nervous than he could remember being since his first date when he was a teen. "It's not even a date, dammit," he mumbled to himself, annoyed when the butterflies ignored him and continued their acrobatic assault of his stomach. He slung his backpack over one shoulder before looking down the street to where he knew Rhys's home and office were. Finally, when he couldn't think of anything else to do, he pocketed his keys and tugged the cuff on his left wrist, wishing he could think up a decent excuse to back out—not that his heart would let him if he tried.

Giving the door a frown, he stepped inside. He paused in the doorway to let his eyes adjust to the dimmer lighting. Once he was certain he wouldn't trip on anything, he headed to the counter to get his coffee. He waited in line for his turn and debated between the chocolate cheesecake brownie and an apple-strudel muffin bigger than his fist. Both were calling his name, he was sure of it.

"Chase?"

He turned at the sound of his name and smiled before he thought about it. Rhys sat at one of the small tables, two drinks, a muffin, and a brownie in front of him. "Some of that for me?" he teased.

"Yep, so get over here before your drink gets cold." The wide grin on Rhys's face calmed him even as the heated look in his eyes stirred his body.

As he walked over to the table, he made sure to put a little extra sway to his hips and gave Rhys his best smile. "Mmm, which one's for me, hun," he purred. "Or do you plan to torment me by eating both, Sayer?"

Rhys chuckled. "That one's for you," he said, motioning to the cup farthest from him. "The Goth-looking barista up there said it was what you usually get."

He sat across from Rhys, inordinately pleased over having coffee and treats waiting for him. "Gabe?"

Rhys grumbled, the scowl accompanying the sound making Chase inexplicably happy. Was the man really jealous of the very straight, very taken coffee boy? *Sweet!* Deciding to not poke the Rhys bear for once, he raised his brow and asked, "And the nummies?"

"I wasn't sure which you would like better, so I got one of each. Your choice."

Chase pondered the man as he thought about which bakery item he wanted. They both looked so good. Instead of picking one, he reached out and carefully broke each in half, placing a piece of each on a napkin. "There. That looks better."

"Creative solution." The chuckle from the other side of the table pleased him more than he thought it should.

He raised his fingers and carefully licked the tips clean with slow, teasing motions. The heat in Rhys's eyes flared white hot, making him wonder how fast they could get back to Rhys's place.

"God, sweetheart." Rhys groaned and stared down at the table intently. "There are laws against things like that in public, or there ought to be."

He laughed, pleased with how thoroughly he affected Rhys. "I'll be good. I promise."

"Yes, you are, sweetheart. Now, eat up and behave."

Chase fake pouted at him, but nibbled at his food, taking sips of his cappuccino every so often.

After a few minutes of quiet eating, he spoke again. "So, you asked me to breakfast so we could talk, but you don't seem to be saying anything, hun. What gives?"

Rhys sat back in his chair, clutching his coffee as if maybe hoping it would protect him somehow. After another moment or two, he looked up, and their eyes met and locked. "I know I have a bad track record with you, but I meant what I said yesterday."

Chase took a moment to sip his peppermint mocha cappuccino and consider what Rhys might be referring to. They had said a great many things to each other over the course of the day, starting from when they awoke in each other's arms to when Rhys walked away after their last dance. "Meaning what?"

"Not about to make any of this easier on me, are you?"

With a smirk, he shook his head. He laughed when Rhys's frown turned into a full-out glower. "Uh-uh. And nope, the man grunt won't work either."

"Ass."

"Yep, and it's a sexy one too. Don't you think?"

"You're gonna make me say it, aren't you?" Rhys asked, not taking the bait. "Fine. I want to properly date you. Take you out. Do things together…. Date." The last sounded more like a question than a statement.

Chase considered all the possible answers he could give, still not completely sold on them being together. "I don't usually give second chances, and we work together, so I'm a little concerned about when this goes wrong."

"When?"

"So far you've insulted me, degraded me, shunned me, and ignored me. Oh, and let's not forget lied to and about me."

"I said I was sorry about that. I won't keep saying it. You have to either forgive me or not, but there were a few things going on at the time that caused my part of the problem."

"You never told me why you acted like such a creep that night, but unless it's germane to the future, I won't ask." He paused to see if Rhys would say anything. Honestly, it bugged the hell out of him, but he wouldn't push.

"I had just thrown Garrett out. Cheating and I don't mix."

"And he looked just enough like me to have you acting like a total ass?" Cheating? Why the hell would someone cheat on a guy like Rhys? Not that he had any patience with cheaters in the first place… but on Rhys? "Yeah, I can see it," he added, not liking the implications or Rhys's ex. "After meeting him, I'd hate me too."

The grunt his comment received made him laugh. "Fair enough. I'm not going to deal with your ex, though. He comes sniffing around again, and he'll find out exactly how little I tolerate little boys like him."

"Somehow, I have a feeling you don't lose." Rhys smirked and shook his head. "I don't think he'll try that again. Not after last time. But I have no interest in ever seeing him again."

"You sure?" He had to ask, though it made him a little sick to do so. However, after Rhys screaming that slut's name instead of his, yeah, he had to ask.

Rhys's brows pulled together as he stared intently at Chase. "Uh, yeah. Real sure. That day he showed up was the first time I'd seen him since the night I caught him with some trick and threw him out."

"Caught?" That was even worse than being cheated on.

He nodded, a pinched look on his face. "In my bed," Rhys mumbled.

"Wait, he brought home some guy to *your* place? That's... I don't know, what's beyond sick?"

"Mm... agreed. Made Mark happy, though."

Happy? What the hell! "That makes no sense, but a lot of other things suddenly do."

"No getting pissed at Mark. He wanted me to dump Garrett months before that happened. Mark hated him."

"Me too, hun. Me too."

He laid a hand over Rhys's, pleased when, instead of pulling away, Rhys turned his over, curling his fingers loosely around Chase's. "Thank you for telling me. I know this was hard for you." The shrug Rhys gave amused him. Never could just man up and out with the feelings. "Now, I have a few rules for you if we're really going to do this thing."

"Rules?" Rhys asked, and then laughed. When Chase merely nodded, he sobered and leaned forward. "You're serious?"

With another nod, he began his short list. "My name or a pet name if you prefer, but no previous lover's name. Ever. Punctuality is a must. If you can't make it, let me know. Oh, and I don't share."

"Anything else?" Rhys asked, the look on his face a cross between amusement and confusion.

Chase thought about it for a moment. Was there? "Nope," he said and smiled. "You?"

Rhys shook his head. "I've never had anyone give me rules before."

Chase's cell rang, drawing his attention. He held up one finger, pulled it out, and checked the screen. *James?* Clicking the accept button, he answered, "Hey, hun? Aren't you and stud-boy supposed to be in bed, not coming up for air for the next week or something? What's up?"

"I've got a five-minute reprieve," James quipped, his voice bubbly and happy as Chase hadn't heard it before. "But I had to call you to let you know our news!"

"It's Sunday. What possible news could you have?" *Did neither man know what a honeymoon was for?*

"Yeah, well, we only just got the news that Danni's grandparents dropped the custody suit. Finally. Seth is over the moon happy, as am I."

The rustling of cloth and murmuring in the background distracted Chase for a moment, but then what Jamie said sank in. "Wait, dropped as in no more courts, social services, et cetera?"

"Yep! Can't believe it. It's been so long we've been fighting to keep our little girl, and now they decided to drop the suit." James's voice dropped to a whisper as he continued. "Wish I could adopt her, but Wisconsin won't allow gay second-parent adoptions."

"I know, but this is great news. When you get back, we'll all have to go out to celebrate!"

Someone tapped Chase on the shoulder, startling him out of the conversation. He blinked and looked up to see Rhys leaning over the table. "What's going on? What was dropped?"

"Hold on, Jamie," he said. "The custody battle for Danni, that's what. Isn't that great?"

Rhys jumped out of his seat so fast, Chase lost track for a moment. He scooped Chase up in his arms and swung him around. "Yes! That's wonderful."

"You wanna put me down now?" he asked, thrilled for James, Seth, and Danni. He was secretly pleased at how easily Rhys could pick him up, even if the coffee shop wasn't the best place for such actions.

"Oh, sorry." Rhys set him on his feet before returning to his seat, grinning the whole way. His cell was out before he managed to get butt to chair.

"Is that Rhys?" James asked.

"Yeah," he sighed. "We grabbed coffee and a snack and were talking when you called. He's telling Dal and who knows who else."

"Great! We'll call a few more people, but I really want to focus on my husband." James laughed, then sighed. "Still can't believe he's really my husband."

"I know, but he is, and I'm so freaking happy for you. Now, go sex your man, or let him sex you. However that works for you two, and enjoy your time away. You deserve to be happy."

"So do you, Chase," James countered.

"I am," he snapped. He took a breath, annoyed with his outburst.

"Chase? What's wrong? I thought things were good with you and Rhys."

"They are. Forget I said that?"

James laughed loudly. "Just promise to be careful and talk to him. I still don't know what set you off last time, but I really do think he'd be good for you. And you for him."

"I know, and I'll try. Now, shoo. Go do sexy things while we finish our rules listings and I get more caffeine."

"Yes, dear, go give your obligatory prayers to the Goddess Caffeina. Love you."

"Love you too," he replied, then clicked "end." Chase waited while Rhys finished his call, then grinned.

"Looks like today is a good day for the future, huh?" Rhys gave him a meaningful look, which Chase failed to ignore, making him squirm in his seat.

"Seems so. Now, did you have any rules to add?"

"Don't think so." He looked down at Chase's empty cup and bare napkin. "You 'bout done?"

"Yeah. Scared you off already?" *My rules shouldn't bother him.*

The deep, rumbling laugh soothed his suddenly tight nerves. "No, sweetheart. I thought we could go for a ride together. I know you rode your bike," he continued, gesturing to the helmet on the seat beside him.

"Yeah, guess I did. Wait, you want to ride with me? On *my* bike?"

Rhys nodded and grinned. "It's not as nice as my Softail, but it's still a sweet bike. So yeah, why not?"

"Just surprised me. No need to get feisty."

Rhys tended to their trash, and in moments they headed out the door and toward Chase's metallic blue Sabre.

WHEN THEY stopped by Rhys's, he ran inside and in moments came back outside, thermos safely ensconced in the backpack he carried. He paused at the sight before him. He'd seen Chase on his bike before, and it never failed to heat his blood. In a leather coat and boots, straddling his bike, Chase was drool-worthy—sex and fire wrapped up in one well-hung and handsome package. Rhys wasn't sure if this was the best or worst idea he'd had in years.

"Well, come on, Rhys," Chase purred, shifting to pat the seat behind him. Really, it was more of a caress, and it had him suddenly hard and needy again. "I can't ride you, I mean, ride with you, if you stand all the way over there."

Oh God, he was in trouble. Chase scooted forward a little as Rhys prowled toward him. "I don't bite," he continued, flashing a half-lidded stare that had Rhys hurrying to climb on behind the slight man now taunting him. "Much," he added with a deep, sexy chuckle.

"My shoulder begs to differ." He reached up to touch the neat dental impression Chase had gifted him with, thankful it was low enough no one saw it unless he stripped off his shirt.

Chase revved the motor and shifted his hips, rubbing his ass against Rhys's groin, drawing a groan from him. "Are you complaining?"

"Never," he said and wrapped his arms around Chase's waist.

"Good." Chase pulled out of the drive, merging with traffic and taking off, though he had no idea where they were going.

Rhys decided it didn't really matter where, he was enjoying spending time with Chase. The fact he could touch the sweet yet prickly man he'd been lusting after for months was an added bonus. One he decided not to waste.

When they approached the waterfront, he tapped Chase's shoulder and pointed, guiding them to one of the small parks along the banks where you could walk out into the water, if you were crazy enough to put one toe into Lake Michigan in the spring.

Chase shifted but didn't move to pull away. "Why are we here?"

He smiled, amused at how Chase looked around the deserted park. "It's a quiet place. We can hang together and drink a little more coffee." He stood and moved a step away, not intending to allow Chase any farther away than necessary.

"Uh, I don't see a coffee shop close."

"Ah, as to that," Rhys said and took off the pack he wore. He dug inside and produced a large thermos of coffee, individual packets of sugar, and portable creamer pods. Digging a little more, he finally pulled out two mugs and presented his goodies to Chase.

Chase gaped at him for a moment before snapping his jaw shut. "You.... You brought us coffee? Seriously?" he asked.

"Chase with no coffee? Um, no. That's dangerous, and we both know it. Now, why don't we go over there," he explained, gesturing to a grassy area near some trees. "We can sit, chat or not chat as the mood hits ya."

The smile Chase gave him made him extraordinarily happy he'd thought of the coffee and the park. Most guys he'd dated would have hated such a simple outing, but he'd thought—hoped—Chase would like it.

Rhys walked to one of the trees and sat, using it for a backrest. Moments later, Chase sauntered over—it was the only way to describe how he moved—and used his boot to force Rhys's legs apart.

"Uh, what are you doing?"

"Getting comfy," Chase cooed. He proceeded to push against Rhys, scooting until they were so close he could feel the bite of his zipper as Chase pushed into his already hard dick. "Ahh... perfect," he added and settled against Rhys's chest.

Torn between wanting to spin Chase around and devour him, and wrapping his free arm around his waist, he decided the cuddle would be best. Besides, what the position made him want was best left behind closed doors.

chapter thirteen

"STILL CAN'T believe he talked me into a first date. I mean, isn't this a bit bass-ackwards? We've already been together a couple of times and *now* he asks me out?" Chase paced in his bedroom, irritated at not being able to calm down. The date was a formality, wasn't it? They already knew they liked each other, though the getting to know each other part was a sweet idea.

"What about this?" Simon asked, ignoring Chase's meltdown. He held up a pair of low-waist herringbone slacks and a heather gray turtleneck cashmere sweater. "Wear this with a pair of your cute little boots, and he'll be putty in your hands."

Chase paused midstep to look at his friend, the huge smile worth any amount of teasing. Simon had been quieter than normal lately, and while he knew why—Si hated being single, and his ex had hurt him badly—it didn't make watching him suffer any easier. "Thanks, Si, and I'm sure you're right. Of course he'll be that anyway," he teased. "I plan to make him have to work for any happy time tonight."

"That's my boy. Now, where's he taking you?"

"Not sure exactly. He said dinner and to the theater, but I'm not sure if he means a movie or downtown to an actual show. I'm kind of hoping it's the latter, though. There are supposed to be some great shows going on, and I haven't been in ages."

"Then we'll hope your bad boy biker cleans up well," Simon said, laughing by the end.

He knew Simon didn't have the best opinion of Rhys, but he was positive once they got to know one another, they'd be friends. "From what

97

I saw at the wedding reception, Rhys cleans up *very* well and is rather educated in culture."

"Really?"

"Simon! You saw him at the reception, the same as I did, and he certainly can fill out a tux." Chase sighed as he thought about how sexy his man had looked in that tux. He just wished he could have helped him back out of it.

"True, true. Still, he just doesn't seem the high-society type." Simon sat up on his bed and started ticking off points on his fingers. "Biker. Huge. Leather. Gruff. Huge. Can bench press my car. Huge."

Chase made it just past the second "huge" before losing his composure and giggling so hard he ended up sprawled beside Simon. "Size and refinement have nothing to do with one another. Besides, he's not that big, Si," he choked out, and slapped Si on the arm.

"Oh," Simon said in mock sincerity. "I'm sorry for you, then, dear."

Chase laughed harder, tears streaming down his face until he finally managed to calm down some. "Oh God, how I love you. If we're going with girth, then I take back my not big statement. 'Cause day-um, he's got more than enough down there to make me wish I enjoyed bottoming."

"Don't tell me things like that when I don't have anyone to play with." Simon pulled the edges of his lips down and he got a faraway look in his eyes.

"Hey, stay with me here. No going into mopey Si mode."

Simon looked at him and smiled, or tried to at least. "I'm fine. Now, go get dressed. You want me to stay and be your chaperon?"

Chase laughed but thought the idea sounded good—not for the reason Si thought, though. He collected his clothes and hurried to the bathroom. "Make yourself comfortable, and I'll be out in a few," he called over his shoulder.

Once the door closed, he set his clothes on the counter and pulled his cell from his pants pocket. He turned on the shower and hit the number for Dale, and then he waited for the call to go through.

"Hey," Dale said, his voice bubbly.

"Hi, Dale. I need your help a minute."

"Sure. What's up?"

"Can you meet me at my apartment in the next"—he paused and checked the time—"half hour? I don't want to leave Si like he is right now."

"Oh, no. Back to pensive and pouty again, is he?"

"A little, but I'm hoping he snaps out of it fast."

"Yeah, be there in a bit."

"Cool, have to get ready fast now. TTFN." Once he set the phone down, he hopped in the shower and cleaned up quickly, hoping the sound had drowned out his conversation.

When he entered the living room, he found Simon playing his PlayStation, sprawled out on the floor, killing evil Templars. "Make yourself at home," Chase teased.

Simon grunted, not taking his eyes off the TV.

"Having fun?"

"Uh-huh."

"I'm thinking of wearing a pink tutu tonight," Chase continued, wondering if Si actually realized he was there.

"That's nice."

He stepped in front of the game. "Si?"

"Hey!" Si snapped. He tapped at the controller before finally looking up to glower at Chase. "What are you doing?"

"Me? I'm getting ready to go out with my… whatever Rhys is. What are you planning to do?" he asked, gesturing at Simon's current position on the floor.

"Well, I *was* playing a game, that's what. Why?" he asked, his tone wary.

"Rhys will be here any min, hun." At Si's downcast eyes, Chase grasped at what to do about his friend. "You wanna stay here?"

"I, um…." Simon trailed off.

"It's cool. The spare room's all yours." The knocking at the door startled them both. Chase looked down at himself, making sure he was ready and satisfied with how his clothes fit, then headed to the door. When he opened it, Dale and Rhys were there.

"Uh, hi," Chase said, concerned at the frown marring Rhys's handsome face.

"Si here?" Dale asked, sauntering past them.

"Why's he here?" Rhys asked, his tone more drawn than the look in his eyes.

"Hold that thought. Let me say g'night, and we can be off. 'Kay?"

Rhys nodded, clearly confused but, thankfully, cooperative.

Chase hurried back to where Dale and Si sat, arguing over which game to play next. "Boys? We're going out now. Don't stay up too late and play nice."

They turned and glowered up at him. "You're so funny, babe. Now, why don't you go have fun with your hunk and leave us to kill bad guys," Dale said. "I brought snacks and everything," he added, patting a blue tote sitting beside him.

"All right, all right. I'm going." He grabbed his jacket on the way out, grumbling about it being his apartment, not theirs. Both men ignored him.

He reached Rhys and exited, pulling Rhys with him. "Come on, you promised me a nice night."

He paused a moment to take in his date: a deep blue button-down tucked into a pair of sleek dress slacks that hugged him beautifully. Rhys even wore a dinner jacket and a silver-striped blue tie. *Yummy!*

"Uh, yeah, but what was all that, and why are they still inside? They don't live with you. Right?"

Chase laughed at the thought. Yeah, so not happening! "No, they don't. Dale is there to keep Si from getting too...." He rolled his hand as he thought how to finish. "Gloomy?"

"Gloomy? What? Is he Eeyore or something?"

He giggled at the idea and that Rhys would compare his friend to a depressed animal in a children's book. Though now he thought about it, it did seem apropos. "No, the ex ran into him recently, flaunting his new boyfriend and claiming his new toy was his one true love and how he'd finally found someone worthy of his love and fidelity. Si's real torn up about it."

"It doesn't sound like you liked the ex."

"Didn't, but Simon refused to listen to us when we warned him the guy was a player and would hurt him." Chase thought about the night Si had first stayed over after that horrible day. "How the man can be such a kick-ass matchmaker and romance author, but not be able to find his own HEA...." he mused, shaking his head. *Seriously, a happily ever after shouldn't be so hard for him.* "I just don't get it, but that's our Si," he added and shrugged.

"So he's crashing with you?" Rhys asked, a small smile bringing out the little laugh lines around his deep emerald eyes. "That's nice of you."

Heat rushed down his neck and up his cheeks. "Thanks," he mumbled, not meeting Rhys's eyes. "He'll be fine. Now, you gonna tell me where we're going?"

"Nope." He led Chase outside to a sleek white and blue Trans Am. He opened the door, held it until Chase was seated, then closed it and headed around the car. Chase leaned over and popped the door for Rhys before settling back into his seat and buckling the belt.

Half an hour later, they pulled into the Milwaukee Center underground parking area. In a few minutes Rhys parked, and they were standing outside The Rep—the Milwaukee Repertory Theater. Chase looked up at the sign and gaped. "You're taking me to the theater-theater? Really?"

"Actually, we're going to the Stackner Cabaret first and then to the theater. We even have reservations," he added, the smile clear in his deep voice.

"Sweet, hun. By the way, whose car did we ride over in?" He had never seen the Trans Am; though, come to think of it, he'd never seen Rhys drive anything but his Harley.

"Mine," Rhys rumbled, the word marred by the heavy laughter. "Where'd you think I got it?"

"Dunno. Just never saw you in a car. Well, one I didn't know, anyway, though I suppose with our weather here, you'd have to have one," he added with a shrug.

"I've had it two, maybe three years. Dal hates it, insisting his Mustang is better, but who doesn't love KITT?"

"Rhys," Chase countered as they stepped inside and up the escalator to the second floor. "KITT was a black Trans Am, not a white and blue one."

"Just be glad I didn't have the blinky light in the front installed like I wanted to."

"Oh God, and you would too. Should have known you were a closet geek!"

Chase squealed when Rhys dug his fingers into Chase's side. "Am not. KITT was cool. Now, be a good boy so we don't get thrown out before dinner."

Biting the inside of his cheek, he nodded and worked to calm the smirk he knew he sported as they entered the restaurant.

DESPITE TWO hours of great music, what held him spellbound was Chase. Rhys watched Chase more than the show, loving how into it he got. The wide grin and swaying of Chase's body in his seat as the music and show played enthralled him. He'd been worried about picking the rowdy Harlem Renaissance musical revue *Ain't Misbehavin'*, but now that he saw Chase loving it so much, he thought maybe they'd have to come more often.

When the last song finished and the lights rose, Rhys wasn't ready for it to be over.

"Oh my God! I loved it. Thank you." Chase threw his arms around Rhys, pulled him down to meet him with eager lips, kissing him like there was no one else there.

Rhys, however, was painfully aware of the people around him, jostling to get their coats and such before heading out. He pulled back and kissed Chase on the tip of his pert little nose. "Glad you liked it so much, sweetheart. Come on, I think we're in the way."

Chase grumbled but agreed, and slipped his arm through Rhys's on the way outside. "That was so cool. I love music of all kinds."

"You're welcome, but the night's not quite over yet." He led the way, Chase tight against him as they walked outside.

"What else did you plan, Rhys?" Chase asked as they reached the car.

"A light snack, then maybe we could go back to my place." He held up a carryout bag he'd stopped to pick up on the way out of the theater.

The bistro catered desserts and drinks to the theater patrons, a fact he was rather thankful for right then.

"More food? As if the wonderful meal before the show wasn't enough? I mean, I have never had roasted butternut squash soup that delicious before. Not even when James made it for me! And I think I'm going to have to hit the gym extra this week over the triple chocolate mousse we had for dessert."

Rhys smiled down at Chase and shook his head, amused by the logical rambling of his lover. "It's not heavy—the snack I mean—and I have no intention of returning you to your friends yet."

"Ah, going to feed me before trying to ravage me?" Chase asked and then slipped into the passenger side of Rhys's baby.

When he reached for his door, it was already unlocked. Rhys hopped in and leaned over the center, so close to Chase he could feel the heat but not the flesh. "Thank you, sweetheart."

"Huh? For what?" Chase murmured, his lips ghosting along Rhys's.

"For the door, for saying yes, take your pick," he explained, then took Chase's lips in a soft, gentle kiss. Instead of pushing to deepen, as he usually would, he traced the tip of his tongue along the seam of Chase's lips, flicking and teasing the silver ring there.

Chase moaned, pushing into the kiss, and swept his tongue along Rhys's, tangling with his and plunging in repeatedly. In mere moments, the kiss went from sweet to mind numbing. He was so enthralled in Chase and his wicked tongue that he jumped, banging his head against the roof when someone blew their horn.

Rhys settled against the seat, focusing on his breathing and his heart rate, trying to calm down so he could drive Chase back to his place. Chase did the same, drawing an amused yet frustrated chuckle from him. "I don't think it's working," he finally said.

"Huh? What's not working?" Chase asked, his voice soft, eyes closed tight.

"Trying to ignore each other," he commented, then put the keys in the ignition and started the car. He forced himself to focus on the area around them instead of how needy the scent of Chase and the Antaeus he always wore made him. After another moment, he pulled out of the parking spot and drove across town.

Chase stayed quiet on the way, but shortly before Rhys pulled into the drive, he rested his left hand on top of Rhys's on the gearshift. He threaded his fingers between Rhys's but did nothing else, following his movements when he shifted gears.

Rhys only relinquished Chase's hand long enough for them to exit the car. As soon as he was around the car and to Chase, he took the long, tapered fingers into his own. With Chase in one hand and their snack in the other, he led them inside and up to his apartment. However, instead of having the treat and hoping to entice Chase to bed, he found himself slammed against the door, Chase's hands tight in his hair, yanking his head down.

Chase mashed their mouths together in a hard, bruising kiss, picking up right where they'd left off in the car. He was moaning in seconds, desperate for the lithe body rubbing against him.

He took a handful of Chase's cheeks and lifted, holding Chase at just the right height to align their cocks through their dress pants. Rhys rocked, thrusting against Chase, torturous and slow, as he groaned and panted.

Chase tore his mouth away from Rhys's with a deep groan. "Oh God, Rhys! Please tell me this can wait," he panted, pointing at the bag on the floor beside them.

Rhys nodded, a grunt all he could manage. He used his grip on Chase to grind against him.

"Bed, now, or I'm going to take you right here, against the wall."

The idea actually gave him pause. Did he want rough sex or to take their time in the big bed? Then his brain kicked in and reminded him he didn't have supplies anywhere but his room. Taking one last kiss, he set Chase down, then dragged him to the bed. All he could think about was Chase getting in him…. Now!

He trembled as Chase stopped next to the bed, hand on his chest. "Calm down, Rhys. I promise to love you like no one ever has before, but I don't want to hurt you either. Strip and get in the center of the bed. Hands and knees, please."

Rhys had no idea what Chase had planned, but nearly came from the heated look alone before he managed to free himself from his clothing and do as ordered.

IT WOULD take him days to recover fully from Chase's rough, driving assault on his hole and cock, but lying awake later, sore and exhausted, he smiled, remembering Chase's promise. He'd been true to his word. No one had ever touched him, or filled him, like Chase had. A fact that both thrilled and terrified him, but one he wouldn't change for anything.

He curled around his sleeping partner, knowing his heart was lost, hoping it wasn't alone.

chapter fourteen

RHYS WISHED they hadn't wasted all this time dancing around one another. Silence had never bothered him until recently, but not having Chase's perky chatting or music going left him on edge. The worst part, and he knew it, was he'd done this to himself by not telling Chase the truth earlier. But if wishes were horses....

A loud ringing interrupted his internal musing. He tapped his Bluetooth—thank you, Chase—and heard the voice say, "Incoming, Mark."

"Accept." Once he heard the cell pick up, he said, "Hey, Mark. What ya up to tonight?"

"Nothing good, man. Is Chase there with you?"

"No, I just dropped him at his place. Why?"

"Can you come into the office? We have a new case to deal with and I need you, sans Chase."

"O… kay." Something was off, but Rhys couldn't place it. After so many years together as friends, first as Marines, then as business partners, he just "knew" something wasn't right. "What aren't you telling me, Mark?" he asked as he pulled over, not wanting to have this conversation while driving.

"The victim's name is Michael Donogual. The same Michael Chase dated. If what I'm finding is right, they broke up not long before you two met. And either it's a setup, or this guy was obsessed with Chase."

The tension in Mark's voice had the hair on his arms and the back of his neck rising. "Define obsessed."

"Like creepy-stalker-woohoo-type obsessed. Like has-a-freaky-shrine-in-his-bedroom obsessed."

Clutching his fist tighter, Rhys struggled to remain calm—or at least calm-ish. "How are you at the scene so fast, and are we officially being hired on this one too?"

"Man, one of the cops that first responded to the call gave the roommate our card. He, in turn, gave it to Michael's parents, so yeah, we're officially adding this to our not-a-suicide case list. I'm wondering how many more there might be, considering we only know of these because of a buddy from when we were in the Corps being a cop now and passing along some information. But I don't think you can ask Chase to do the computer work on this one, Rhys. Not if what I'm hearing about is anything like what will be on this guy's laptop, desktop, or numerous other gadgets found so far." Mark paused a moment before continuing. "I'm still surprised we're even getting the level of cooperation we are."

Rhys sat motionless, afraid if he spoke right then his voice would give out. No, he couldn't ask Chase to work on this one, not if this guy was one of his exes. He just hoped no one would say anything to Chase until after he could talk to him.

"We'll figure something out and just be thankful for contacts and friends. Do me a solid, though, okay? Don't mention this to Chase, and let Nikki and such know to keep a tight lid on things for now. I don't want him alone when he finds out."

"No problem. I wouldn't want to be the one to tell him, ever, if it were possible. He's going to lose it," Mark added matter-of-factly. "I know I would."

Rhys sighed, not looking forward to that discussion, but thankful he would get the chance to be the one there for Chase. Now to hope he didn't kill the messenger.

The two men divided the initial work before saying good-bye. Rhys prayed James, Seth, and Chase would miss the news until after he could get things started and return to Chase.

"THAT'S NOT…." Rhys trailed off, looking away again.

Chase had never seen Rhys so nervous or unsure of himself. It suddenly occurred to him there might be a lot more depth to the man than he had thought. Then he scolded himself for assuming the wrapping was all there was to Rhys. He hated when people made the assumption about him, yet here he was doing the same. *Idiot.* "What is it? I can handle it, whatever it is." Or he hoped so, at least.

Rhys took another sip of his coffee before he reached over and took Chase's hand. When their eyes met, Chase was suddenly afraid to hear whatever it was Rhys didn't want to say. "I don't want to tell you what you need to be told, but it should come from someone who cares about you."

"Okay...." Chase paused. It had been weird enough to have Rhys show up at his front door first thing in the morning, but this? Yeah, this he didn't like, especially not with that for an intro. "Now you're scaring me, Rhys. What happened? Wait, it's not James, is it? Please tell me nothing happened to Jamie!"

"No." Rhys stood and went around the coffee table to hold Chase as he started to come undone. "I'm sorry, sweetheart. Forgive me for messing this all up. It's not James. He's fine." He continued to offer comfort and eventually Chase calmed.

"Then what is it? And don't ever scare me like that again!"

"Sorry."

Chase took a deep breath. Rhys's fidgeting and refusal to meet his eyes scared him. "Just tell me, please. I can't stand this."

"There's been another death, and this time you know the person. Or at least you did. The cops believe it was a staged murder this time, but we've been hired by the family to make sure."

Chase's voice broke as he whispered, "W-who died?"

"Michael Donogual."

"Mikey?" he choked out.

Rhys scooped Chase up into his arms and cuddled him in his lap where he sat on the couch, rubbing circles on his back. Right then Chase wished James were there too. They had been each other's lifelines for so long, it felt weird to seek comfort in someone else instead of his best friend.

Eventually he calmed, though the tears didn't stop completely, nor did the pain lessen. "What happened?"

"We're not sure yet. What we do know, though, is he had a large amount of alcohol and drugs in his system."

Chase shook his head. "No, that can't be right. You've got it wrong."

"Sweetheart, I assure you, every word is right. His parents have already ID'd his body."

"No, Mikey barely drank and never took drugs. Hell, he'd barely take a damn aspirin, Rhys."

"Chase," Rhys said, his voice deep and soothing. "I understand that. I didn't say it was logical, just what was found. The fact he had a large amount of GHB in his system makes sense if it were murder, unless he really was suicidal."

At the mention of the "s" word, Chase froze again. He knew that was the MO of the psycho doing this, but oh God! "H-how did he die?"

"Slit his wrists in the bath. Though he may have actually…."

He couldn't hear anything else said, his mind spinning and sticking on the word "wrists." His eyes flicked down to the wrist cuff he wore. The cuff that was identical to the one he kept in his lock box. That one had been Ethan's before…. Before that horrible day….

Chase had been with friends at the mall, hanging out and eating crap his mom would kill him for if she knew. His cell had lit up while they were in a movie, and he'd hit End quickly, not wanting to deal with whining patrons or grumpy words just 'cause he'd forgotten to turn the thing off.

When he exited the mall later that afternoon, he'd switched his phone back on. When he checked the missed call, it was Ethan and there was a voice mail. *Cool.*

Moments later, he heard E's voice. "I can't take it anymore, Chase. I just can't! Dad did it again, screaming how he was going to beat the gay out of me." His voice broke, and Chase could hear him crying before he whispered, "If he doesn't kill me next time, he's going to send me to one of those reprogramming camps. Please forgive me."

Chase stood by his car, frozen for a moment until his brain kicked in. He'd jumped into the car and sped across town, hoping to get to Ethan before he did something stupid, or worse… permanent. About a block away from Ethan's house, lights flashed behind him and a siren chirped, but he kept going. No way was he going to lose his cousin, his brother really, to hate and prejudice because he stopped on his way there!

He parked half on the curb, threw his door open, and sprinted into the house, screaming for Ethan. He knew someone was chasing him, but he didn't care if it was some cop or one of E's parents. All he knew was he had to get to Ethan before it was too late.

Someone grabbed his arm, but he shook them off, tearing into Ethan's bedroom. Empty! He looked around, terrified, and noticed the bathroom door, cracked. Blind fear gripped him, and he bolted through the door. Moments later, he knelt on the wet floor, screaming, "Ethan!"

"Chase!" Rhys bellowed, yanking him out of the nightmare that had been his teen years.

Not able to completely shake the memories or sense of crushing loss, he curled against Rhys's broad chest and cried for Ethan, for Michael. His throat hurt, and he was so tired he could barely think.

He must have dozed off at some point, because he became aware the light was all wrong and he lay atop Rhys on the couch. The man's powerful arms were still wrapped around him tightly.

"Cariadon?" Rhys's voice was gentle, like an adult might speak to a terrified, small child. "You with me again?"

Chase nodded, but didn't speak yet. Would Rhys be disgusted? Irritated?

Chase felt the huge sigh he let out. "Thank you," Rhys rumbled. "Chase, where'd you go earlier?"

"To a time I'd rather forget," he mumbled into Rhys's shoulder.

"And Ethan?"

"Best friend and cousin growing up, but his parents didn't take to his coming out as well as mine did."

"And how Michael died made you think of your friend?"

Chase heard the curiosity in Rhys's voice, but telling that whole story was beyond him right then. "I can't, Rhys. I'm sorry, but I can't talk about Ethan yet."

"Chase—"

"No, listen to me, if you want to know about Ethan, go ask James. He knows it all. But, please, I can't work on this one. The others were bad enough, but I just can't."

"Shhh…. No one wants you to. I called a friend from my military days. He'll be here later today to help."

"Huh?" Chase looked up, confused. "If you have a buddy who does computer forensics, why'd you get James to con me into working for you?"

"I didn't get him to do anything. If you recall, I wasn't overly happy at the time, though for a different reason than your ire. No, my buddy, Grayson Miles, isn't local. He lives in DC but agreed to help out after I explained the situation."

"Oh. You're not getting rid of me, are you?" he asked, knowing his outburst and tears had likely freaked Rhys out. The last person who'd found out some of the details of Ethan and that time of his life dumped him over it.

"No, dear. A soaked T-shirt or two won't *chase* me off."

"Not funny," he grumbled and swatted the chest he still sprawled across. "I'll let your friend have access to the stuff he needs, but he has to stay out of my area. At least unsupervised. That's my firm's office area too." Chase sat up so fast he nearly fell. "Oh God. What time is it?"

"Careful. It's, um, almost ten now. But being I'm your boss, I'll forgive you being tardy."

"I have a teleconference at eleven. Dammit," he grumbled, knowing he looked like crap and an hour would not fix how puffy and red his eyes likely were.

"Go get ready. I'll drive us to work, okay?"

"Thanks, Rhys. For everything." He hurried into his bedroom to grab a quick shower and dress to restart the day. Surely, it would all get better from here…. *Right?*

LATER THAT day, Rhys came into his office area, a wary look on his chiseled, handsome face. "Chase?"

It took a moment for him to blink himself out of code and keyboards, but he turned to face Rhys once he could focus on the real world again. "Huh? What's up?"

"You remember my old service buddy is supposed to come today to help you with the murder cases? I wanted to introduce you to him and make sure things were settled before I have to head out for a bit."

Confused at Rhys's nervousness, Chase nodded, assuming it would make more sense later. "Sure. I set him up a workspace already." He looked past Rhys but didn't see anyone waiting. "Um, unless he's invisible, I don't see him."

"He's waiting out front with Nikki. I thought it best to warn you first."

He thought that over, not liking the idea. Was Rhys babying him because he thought Chase couldn't share space or because of his meltdown earlier? Either way, he didn't like the implications. "Why, won't I like him? Is he some homophobic prick or"—Chase smirked up at Rhys, hoping to dispel his worries—"all gross scary looking or something?"

For the first time all day, Rhys cracked a smile. "No, he's neither of those. First off, he bats for our team. Secondly, I'm told many men have thought him quite handsome, though I can't see it." He chuckled. "But you can be a little… territorial about your space, so I thought it best to advise you he'd arrived."

Territorial? Only of his personal systems, friends, and lover. Not over space. Usually. "Okay, bring in Mr. Hot Shot IT. Should be fun to hear about what kind of guy you were in your Marine days." Rhys grumbled something he couldn't hear. "What was that, hun?"

"Nothing. Just be nice."

"I always am," he quipped, though his heart wasn't in it.

Five minutes later, he was back with a somewhat cute guy in tow. Chase did the once-over, checking out his new office mate. Long dark-chocolate-brown hair, light amber eyes, and tall. He was almost as tall as Rhys—maybe six three or four? Thinner build but not a lightweight by any means. The deeply tanned skin and high cheekbones spoke of a Native American heritage, though he wasn't sure which tribe. What caught his attention most was the slight hump to his nose, as if it had been broken a time or two, and the distinctive scar across his left cheek. Altogether, he looked both dangerous and handsome, though not nearly as much as Rhys.

"This is Chase. Chase, this is Miles, and he'll be your tech roomie for now," Rhys said, motioning to each man in turn. "This is Chase's area, so I'll let him show you around and explain what's what."

Chase stuck out his hand and mustered a small smile for the well-dressed man. "Chase Manning."

"Grayson Miles. This one here"—he nodded to Rhys—"still calls me by my last name at times. Also, he tells me you run his IT section and have a consulting firm?"

"I do. You would think computers were strange alien beasts the way he goes on when he needs something 'hard.'"

The man smiled, not showing any teeth, but it looked genuine to Chase. "Yeah, he's always been that way. So, would you mind?" he added as he turned. The wide-eyed stare made Chase smile, a real smile that time. "We never get such nice equipment where I work now," he added, awed.

"You may go, Rhys. I can show him around on my own." It wasn't that he didn't appreciate Rhys trying to lighten his load or being considerate, but he was getting sick of the hovering. He was a grown man and fully capable of being both professional and mature.

Rhys arched his brows but held his tongue, a fact Chase was thankful for right then. He nodded, clasped Grayson on the shoulder, and left the area.

"So, I set you up over here. Rhys didn't tell me what equipment you might bring, but if you need anything more than what's here, let me know, and I'll see what I can do for you."

"Thanks," Grayson said, his voice strong yet soft. The dichotomy of the man was as perplexing as it was confusing. This man was a hardened Marine? "Let me get my things, and we'll see where I need to begin."

"Sure. Come on, I'll help you unload. Ask one of our muscle-bound bosses and no telling what might happen," Chase teased and led the way out front. As he passed the reception desk, Nichelle gave him a small smile and he returned it, but by the sigh and sad look, he figured it hadn't been good enough to relieve her worry.

chapter fifteen

RHYS STOOD out front of James's stone cottage-like home, torn between knocking on the door to find out what he needed to know and turning around. He was a PI, though, and unanswered questions were like an itch under his skin, not something he took to well. Swallowing his indecision, he raised his hand and knocked.

After a few moments, he heard movement and the door opened. James stood before him, little flecks of paint on his hands and the forearm crutches he used. Barefoot and dressed in his usual painting garb of a T-shirt and threadbare jeans, he looked up and smiled. "Hey, Rhys. What brings you by this time of day?"

Well, that question answered whether Chase had let him know about the murder or if he'd offered up Rhys as his storyteller. "Hi, Jay. May I come in?"

"Oh, yeah. Sorry about that." James maneuvered to let him past and then closed the door. "Let's head into the kitchen. Want a drink? I've got coffee, bottled water, or I can make you some tea."

"Water would be fine, thanks." He followed James in, grabbing a bottle of water for each of them before settling on one of the kitchen stools.

James washed up, then took his stool; it had wheels, and no one, not even his stepdaughter Danni, was allowed to use it. "From the dark cloud around you, I'm assuming this isn't a happy visit."

"Haven't caught the news or talked to Chase, huh?"

"No, why?"

He spent the next half hour telling James everything that had happened that morning, including Chase's freak-out and about him screaming "Ethan." Partway through, James asked him to stop talking and sent a series of texts back and forth with someone before motioning Rhys to continue. Once he was done with his retelling of the death and Chase's reaction, Rhys felt drained, and he hadn't even heard the rest yet. He knew he had to find out what Chase had sent him there to hear, though.

"What I don't know, though, is what happened from there. After he found his cousin, I mean. Or what it is he thinks you can tell me. I mean, you didn't meet until college, so I'm a little confused. Beyond that, I'm worried about him."

"No, we didn't, but just as he was my champion, I was his focus for a long time as he fought to become the man you now know." James stared out the back window, eyes unfocused, not speaking for a few minutes. "He told you to ask me about Ethan and the year afterward," he explained, holding his cell up with a sad smile. "Did he tell you how we actually met?"

Rhys shook his head. "College is all either of you has said."

"Mm.... We met at Dr. Wolfe's office. She was the psychologist I went to after I escaped the hell my last year of home was. Chase had been seeing her for a time at that point. Our appointments seemed to coincide often, and eventually, we started chatting while waiting to be called back or for a ride to show up."

"Okay, I get he had a really hard time with not only losing his cousin but being the one to find him. That would mess up anyone."

"Ethan wasn't just his cousin. He was Chase's best friend and confidant." James fidgeted and sighed, his look screaming annoyance. "You're a PI, and you never noticed he always answers his phone? And I do mean *always*. Or that no one ever sees him without his leather cuff. One he has worn every day since before I met him. I figured when I talked you into hiring him, you'd dig a little into his past."

"I did," Rhys snapped, knowing he sounded defensive. "But teen records are sealed, not that I found even those on him."

"Had you known the right things to ask or dug more, you would have found that a couple of months after Ethan died—his entire family blames his uncle to this day, by the way—Chase almost joined him. They call it survivor's guilt."

"I don't get it. Why would he think that? He wasn't even there," Rhys defended, not wanting James to be right.

"That's the point, Rhys. He was too busy watching a movie when his friend and cousin called him, leaving his suicide note on Chase's voice mail. How messed up do you think that made him? If only he had paid more attention to how bad things were for Ethan. If only he had answered the call. If only he had turned the cell back on as soon as he got out of the movie. If only…."

"His cousin's death wasn't his fault," Rhys growled.

"I know that. So does he, now. But that doesn't change how dark his mind went afterward."

Rhys thought about it, his heart hurting. His stomach lurched when he finally settled on the only logic he could find. "Oh God. He wears the cuff to cover his scars, doesn't he?"

James nodded. "Yes, and because they had matching cuffs. Seventeen-year-old boys who felt like the other was the only one that could understand them. You get it?"

"Yeah. I do."

"The fact that same method was used to kill his ex, yeah, that's going to make it that much harder for him." James paused, looking him over carefully. Rhys felt as if the immense weight of the conversation increased tenfold before James spoke again. "The fact he let you comfort him is a major thing. Honestly, I would expect him to have called me, crying, or have tried to drive over. That he told you to come here to ask questions only reinforces things for me. Don't know what you did, but you've definitely gotten to him."

"Normally, I would be thrilled with that news, but right now I'm more worried about him than our unsteady relationship."

"He'll be okay. He sent you here to learn more. It's the only reason I've told you what I have. You are now one of about three people that know, outside his family and old therapist." James reached over, patting Rhys's trembling hands. "Be worthy of his trust, please."

"Three? What about his exes?"

James shook his head. "No. Not that I know of, at least. I doubt any of them even knew about the scars. I mean, he sleeps with that cuff on if anyone other than me is around. You figure it out," he added, his voice a challenge. "He's so strong. Stronger than me in many ways. But he is so very fragile as well. He just rarely lets anyone see that side of him. Take care of him."

"I will, I promise," he swore, knowing it was an oath, not merely a platitude. He would do whatever it took to keep Chase safe, including fighting the demons from his past if need be.

By the time he made it back to the office, having procrastinated as much as he could justify, it was normal closing time. Not that work stopped then, but the office would be locked and the phones switched over to the answering service.

Rhys pulled into his spot at the office, noting Miles's car was still there. He double-checked for Chase's before remembering he'd driven Chase in. *He's probably pissed I wasn't here to take him home... like any logical person would be. Dammit.*

Dismounting, he pulled his helmet off, tucking it under his arm before heading inside, wondering what kind of reception to expect. Chase had a temper, or did with him at least. Instead of the pissed-off cutie he expected, though, he found Miles and Chase still hard at work.

"Um, guys? It's past quitting time for you two." He couldn't believe Mark or Nichelle wouldn't have reminded them—Chase often got lost in his work and had to be reminded to take breaks or stop at the end of the day.

Both men turned, blinking hard, before focusing on him. "Sorry," Chase murmured. "Getting a late start today means I still have a bit more work to do."

"And Mark got me started digging through this thing," Miles grumbled and gestured to a battered, older laptop. "Damn thing has more viruses on it than data," he added with a sneer.

"Find anything?" Rhys asked Miles, eyes flitting to Chase, wary of his stability still.

"Nothing that matches what Mark and you said was found in the apartment. I mean, he seems to have missed Chase after they broke up, but nothing obsessive."

Chase's shoulders sagged, the sigh audible as he deflated at Miles's words.

"Good. Why don't you come to my office and we can discuss it more? Then you can go upstairs to crash. I know you're still tired, and I seriously doubt you're going to make it much longer, man." Noting the annoyance that flashed across Miles's face, he added, "This is stuff his parents gave us access to, so take your time. The cops will have more and will eventually demand this stuff too probably, but not yet."

"All right." Miles stood and walked with Rhys but paused at the doorway to look at Chase. "I don't know if it helps or not, but he didn't do this to himself over you."

He nodded slowly. "Thanks. Go on. Rhys isn't overly patient when he wants answers."

Miles laughed but followed Rhys to his office, who closed the door once they were inside. He settled into his chair and waited as Miles—Grayson dammit, civilian now!—took one of the two chairs on the other side of his desk.

"Do you have anything else on the case yet, and how did Chase do with you in his area?"

"Hm…. As far as me being there, he seemed fine," Grayson said and shrugged. "Even put up with me looking over his shoulder to see what he was working on at one point. And damn, he's as good as his rep, if not better. Cannot believe you got him working here. Seems like a waste of his skills."

"Don't let him fool you. Most of his work is for his consulting firm, not for us. That's actually why he's got so much stuff here and why the computer area is now the back half of the office. He keeps picking up clients, and he's going to need to hire people, but the office space is part of his compensation for his work for the Coiled Dragon."

"He mentioned that earlier." Grayson drummed his fingers as he considered Rhys again. "As for the issue at hand, this Michael guy kept a digital journal. I doubt Chase would like some of what's in there, but it just doesn't back up the staging."

"So nothing to back suicide or obsession?"

118

Grayson shook his head and grunted in the negative. "Man was a bit weird, but the only thing of interest on the laptop or iPad I've found so far is the extensive collection of porn and Yaoi."

"By the way you keep looking away while talking to me, I have to assume there's something else bothering you about his case?" Rhys asked.

"The journal mentioned Chase taking off occasionally for some guy named James. He thought Chase was cheating on him but wasn't sure. I worry about you and if he's the kind of guy to be serious with?" he said, making it a question at the end.

Rhys laughed, amused Grayson thought he needed protecting from Chase and at the idea of James and Chase as a couple. "If there's one person I don't have to worry about him running off with, it's James. James just married Seth Burns and is too blissfully happy to notice anyone else. Besides, they're best friends, not lovers."

Grayson shrugged. "I'm merely relaying what I found."

"Understood, but man, it's more like how when I needed you, you came immediately. Or last year when you asked for help, Dane and I flew out right away, not even asking you why."

"But they're not Marines."

"Trust me, that doesn't matter in this case."

"They that close?"

"Mm…. Yes. Sometime I'll tell you all about it, but suffice to say, James is only a threat to me if I hurt Chase." He smiled as he remembered James's words about how much Chase trusted him. "We're new, but I'm in this for the long haul."

"No poaching. Got it," Grayson quipped and smirked. "Eh, you know he's not my type, Sayer. Besides, I'm not blind. Boy watches you like a mama bear guarding her cub."

Rhys smiled, pleased with the fact his friend had spotted the connection between them so easily.

CHASE WATCHED Rhys lead the new guy, Grayson, to his office. When he heard the door click shut, he pulled out his cell, hit speed dial two, and waited for James to pick up. On the fourth ring, he figured James wasn't near his cell, but then heard his clear, low voice say "Hello."

"Jamie? Thank goodness."

"Yeah, it's me. Rhys make it back to the office yet?"

"Yeah, but he was a little off. Instead of talking to me about the conversation, he's in his office with Grayson, discussing the case." He understood, and would have done the same if he were Rhys, but the fact he'd stood so far away and didn't smile or tease at all bothered him.

"Grayson? Who's that?"

"Some buddy of his from his Marine days. He's also a pretty decent computer guy, from what I can tell. But... come on, James. Don't make me beg. What'd he say when you told him?"

"Not as much as I expected, honestly. He seemed confused and worried mostly," James explained. "But, Chase, why'd you send him to me for the story? You've never wanted me to talk about your past before."

"I've never freaked out on someone like I did this morning, either," Chase grumbled.

"Possibly, but I think it's more. Come on, Chase, spill."

The pleading tone broke him. Only James could do that to him, and the man damn well knew it too. "I feel different about him," Chase mumbled, not wanting to be overheard and not completely certain admitting to how much he cared about Rhys was a good idea.

"Duh. Why the hell do you think we all pushed you together so hard? There has been something between you since the time I saw you stare at him and then run and hide in my kitchen. Even as bad as things were when we met Rhys last year, when my brother was stalking me and sending death threats and all," James said, his voice faltering, "there was something tangible about your energy around each other."

"Pushed together? I get that's why you wanted me to work here, brat," he added fondly. "But who's this 'we all'?"

"Did one date you went on go well after you met Rhys? Think about how good Simon usually is at setting people up. You really think he could mess up that badly every time, without some effort on his part?"

"I'll kill him! You mean he deliberately set me up with assholes?" The nerve! "Wait, but when I went out with Adrian, Rhys was on a date with some boy." A fact that still rankled a bit, but he'd refused to mention before.

"And how do you think he knew where to be and when to make sure you saw him?"

Chase thought that over and frowned, though he knew James could not see him. They had *all* worked to drive him insane and block him from finding someone other than Rhys? He was even more bothered by the fact he felt warmth spread in his chest that they would go to such lengths to help him, even against his wishes and claimed wants.

"Now," James interrupted his rambling thoughts. "Instead of fixating on what we did *for* you, or on the past, why don't you go kick this Grayson guy out of Rhys's office and put down some real roots with the big man?" A deep chuckle came through the line. "Go show him who he belongs to and remind yourself you're both healthy and alive."

"Dammit, Jamie. You're supposed to be the shy, quiet one. I'm supposed to be the outrageous one who suggests things like bending him over his desk."

The chuckle became a full-on belly laugh. "I never said over his desk, dear. That's all yours, though it would look great on canvas...." James trailed off, and seconds later, he realized the call had ended. Chase looked at the phone and grinned. Yeah, he knew what James was off to paint. *Wonder if I can talk him into letting me buy it?*

chapter sixteen

CHASE KNEW Mark and Nichelle were gone for the day, though Mark was probably upstairs in his loft, so it was just Grayson he had to wait out so he could spend time with Rhys. For the first time in years, his initial instinct hadn't been to run to James. Not calling James right away and waiting while Rhys found out about his past was one of the hardest things he'd done in a long time. However, if they were going to be a real couple, with a possibility of a future, he had to be open. Only problem was, he couldn't talk about Ethan. Not yet, maybe never. Thankfully, James had stepped in and rescued him.

He closed down his computer, intending to follow James's suggestion. Truthfully, he had thought of it a few times lately but hadn't wanted to risk being caught having sex by Mark or Nikki. Somehow, that no longer mattered to him. Living his life, however, did. Once he was certain everything was saved and off, he grabbed his pack and went to the reception area to wait. Settling into one of the comfy chairs, he planned his attack, determined to have his way with Rhys. He just hoped Rhys was good with office sex.

A short time later Rhys came out with Grayson, laughing. They made it to the IT area before either man noticed Chase wasn't there. He took the opportunity to ogle Rhys's tight butt and the sensuous way he moved.

After a moment, Rhys turned, searching for him. "There you are."

Chase flashed him a smile. "Yep, finish up with your friend, hun. Changed my mind about staying late."

Rhys's face fell a little, but Chase bit his tongue so as not to give away what he'd planned. "Oh, okay. I'll take you home in just a minute, then."

"No worries."

Grayson and Rhys spoke for a few more minutes while the other man gathered his things. He waited while Rhys walked Grayson out, knowing he would have Rhys at his mercy soon.

Checking the door to make sure he had time, Chase hurried into Rhys's office, set his backpack on one of the chairs, pulled out an individual packet of lube and a condom, then tucked both into the front pocket of his jeans. He looked around, happy Rhys was such a tidy guy. His desk held his computer, a few loose items that were easily moved to safety, and a file folder he carefully placed on top of the closest file cabinet.

Once he was happy with his setup, he sat behind the desk in Rhys's chair and waited. When he heard Rhys come back inside, his pulse spiked and his mind spun with what he intended to do to his man.

"Chase?" Rhys called curiously.

"In here, Rhys," Chase replied, dropping his voice a little.

A moment later, Rhys stood in the doorway, brows pulled together, forehead creased. "What are you doing in here and… hey, where's the stuff I had on my desk?"

Meeting the incredulous man with a heated, heavy-lidded gaze, Chase crooked his finger, motioning Rhys forward. "Shut the door and come here."

"You okay?" he asked but did as told. "What's going on?"

Chase shifted, widening his legs so Rhys stood between them. He reached out and grasped the belt in front of him, unhooking it.

"Uh, not that I don't like you when you're being friendly, but what are you doing?" Rhys asked.

Annoyed he needed to catch Rhys up with the plan, he huffed and stood, forcing the bigger man against the desk. He slipped his hands under the red T-shirt, dragging it up the tight, defined muscles. Once he'd exposed a thin strip of lightly freckled skin, he teased it lightly.

Rhys's groan had Chase's cock hard and throbbing, begging for attention. He ignored it, determined to drive Rhys as crazy as he already drove Chase.

"Chase? Baby?"

Chase tugged on the shirt, annoyed it was in his way. "Off," he mumbled as he dipped his head to leave barely there kisses across Rhys's chest.

Rhys obeyed, much to Chase's silent satisfaction. He rubbed his hands and fully clothed body against Rhys's half-naked one. He reveled in the whimper when he pinched both nipples between his fingers, tugging and twisting, careful not to injure.

"We're still in the office," Rhys panted, pushing into Chase's ministrations.

"Mm… I know." Swiping his tongue across one of Rhys's peaked nipples, he teased and tormented it before sucking it into his mouth hard and carefully biting down and worrying the nub. The groan that slipped out of Rhys had Chase practically giddy, loving how hungry the man always turned in his hands.

"Ohh… my place is just… upstairs," Rhys forced out between moans.

"Don't want to wait. Want to live," Chase countered, tracing his fingers along Rhys's abs, teasing down the light ginger hair that ran from his navel to his groin.

"Live?" Rhys shivered when Chase dipped his fingers beneath the waistband of his jeans, ghosting a touch across the tip of Rhys's cock. The dampness there thrilled Chase even more than the sounds falling from the man's delicious mouth.

"No past." Chase stood on his tiptoes so he could nip along Rhys's collarbone and up his neck. "No future," he added, pulling Rhys down a little more. "Just you, me," he continued before sucking on Rhys's pulse point, "and what we can do together," he finished, and bit down on the spot he'd just teased, hard.

"Ch-Chase…."

He smirked against Rhys's throat, loving how his man trembled for him. "You want more, boy?"

"Not a—"

Chase knew Rhys would argue over the word boy, so he twisted both nipples and bit down again, pleased when Rhys words turned into a low, long moan.

Releasing one tight red bud, he latched on with his mouth as he deftly unbuttoned Rhys's jeans, pushing them and his boxer briefs off his hips. After a moment of fighting with the material, he hobbled Rhys. Chase pulled back and looked his lover over, desperate to be inside *now* but not ready to give up on his torture yet. He took Rhys by the arm, spinning him away so he faced the desk, and pushed down on his shoulders. "You're going to need to hold on tight."

"What are you doing?"

"That should be perfectly obvious," he cooed. He trailed his fingers down Rhys's back and buttocks, loving how his skin goose fleshed and the muscles twitched. He frowned as he realized Rhys was still too tall. "Spread your legs, babe. I'm not getting a ladder to fuck you."

Rhys chuckled, but instead of cooperating, he shifted so quickly Chase was startled when Rhys turned, scooped him up, and laid him out across the desk. "Rhys!" he squeaked, unsure what was going on.

Chase watched in stunned silence as Rhys deftly undid his pants and stripped him, leaving him in nothing but his shirt. He opened his mouth to object but gasped instead when Rhys bent over and licked a path up one thigh. The moan that came out would have embarrassed him if he'd been able to think clearly. Right then, though, he couldn't care about anything but how Rhys touched him.

"I'd love you to fuck me, baby," Rhys rumbled against where his thigh joined his groin. "But later. Right now…." Rhys repeated the same action on the other side, pulling another moan from him. "I think you need to let go and let me love you," Rhys finished, then nuzzled Chase's sac.

"Rhys…."

Rhys traced the tip of his tongue around the head of Chase's weeping cock. Chase propped himself up on one elbow and tangled his hand in Rhys's soft, short hair—not hard enough to hurt, but enough to pull another groan from his lover. Rhys's eyes widened, and his lips parted just enough to suck the head of his cock between them.

Wrapping one large hand around Chase's length, Rhys nursed on his cock, sucking and licking, with just a touch of teeth, making Chase writhe and whimper continuously. When Rhys tightened and relaxed his lips rhythmically, altering the pressure and suction on Chase's rod, Chase keened, trying to warn Rhys. "Clooooose…."

Rhys's eyes twinkled as he met Chase's gaze, taking him deeper and harder, swallowing repeatedly around his tip. A moment later, Chase felt a wet finger slip behind his balls, rubbing along his taint as he writhed and moaned. Rubbing his tongue along the underside of Chase's cock, Rhys hummed, sending him even higher. When Chase felt Rhys's finger massage and probe his hole, he was so far gone and needy, he pushed back instead of pulling away, as he normally would. Rhys pushed inside him, his movements careful as he continued until he managed to hit Chase's happy spot. Chase yelled as Rhys continued to rub and press while sucking harder.

Chase slammed his hands down on the desk, scrabbling for something to hold on to as his back arched. Just before Chase came, Rhys pulled off, stroking him hard and fast until he shot, decorating his chest with his release.

Before he could process what Rhys was doing, the man climbed up onto the desk and knelt over Chase. Chase watched, dazed yet fascinated, as Rhys stroked once, twice, and once more before he roared out his pleasure, adding his spend to what was already on Chase's body. Without thinking, Chase wrapped his arms and legs around Rhys, pulling him down to press his lips against Rhys's in a silent thank-you as he continued to shudder from the power and depth of his need fulfilled.

Minutes later, when his brain kicked on again and his breathing calmed enough so he wasn't afraid he would pass out, Chase shifted under Rhys, frustrated at his lack of space. He didn't really want Rhys to move, though, so he focused instead on caressing Rhys's back, arms, and hips as he waited for his lover to calm and move.

When Rhys finally moved to lift off him, Chase shifted again to help him lie down where he'd just been. Chase watched, entranced, as Rhys rested, his eyes wide and glassy. He pulled a pack of baby wipes from his bag before wiping first himself and then Rhys down.

He quickly donned his clothes and then focused on Rhys again. Using slow, careful strokes, he cleaned Rhys of all traces of their come, kissing and petting him as he went.

"Hun? Rhys?" Chase asked against Rhys's back, his voice soft, awed. "You need help?"

His only answer was the nod from Rhys. Chase pulled the rolling leather chair closer and then helped maneuver Rhys until he was sitting in it, sprawled back, his legs wide. Rhys's strong arms shot out and pulled Chase into his lap.

"Thank you, sweetheart." Rhys nuzzled Chase's damp temple.

Chase chuckled as he snuggled into the wide chest. "You don't need to thank me for that, hun. I think we both enjoyed that."

"No," he rumbled against Chase's skin. "For giving us a chance. For trusting me with your secrets."

"Thank you for not giving up on me."

"Huh?"

"James told me about all the plotting against me." He swatted Rhys's arm. "Including ruining my date with Adrian, you ass."

Rhys grunted.

"Poor guy deserved better than that."

"Can find his own boyfriend. He can't have mine."

"As much as I like the sentiment, hun, I think you might want to move before you stick, permanent-like." He giggled at the indignant grumble, amused at how rough yet sweet the man beneath him was.

Rhys plucked at Chase's clothes, a deep frown on his face. "How come you're dressed?"

Chase ignored the question and instead said, "Don't worry, baby, I think you're yummy like this. Maybe I should keep you naked all the time."

"Yeah, sure, that would go over well come time to work."

"Hmm…. True, they don't all need to see what you've got going on under your clothes. Fine," he sighed. "I supposed you can wear clothes when outside the doors of whichever apartment we're at."

"Gee, thanks. I'm no one's slave boy."

"No, but I like the idea of the easy access. Now hush and get up. I'm hungry, and I haven't eaten all day. Caffeine only goes so far."

"You didn't eat? Why?"

"I, um, couldn't before. Between this morning and worrying about how things would be when you returned from James's, I, well…." He shrugged, unsure how to finish.

"Sweetheart, you can't go without eating."

"The thought of food, ugh."

"But now?"

"James reminded me that life is for the living and that I needed to embrace the life I have, not stay mired in the past."

"Good for him."

"Yep, then he told me to go fuck you over your desk. I'm thinking the man's a genius," he added, grinning. The flush that spread over Rhys's cheeks had him laughing so hard, tears slid down his cheeks.

"It's not that funny."

"Yeah, it is," Chase managed to get out. "Though you did derail my intentions. Have to say, though, I rather like your plan. We'll have to try this again. Soon."

Rhys stood, still holding Chase, and unceremoniously dumped him in the chair. Chase watched as Rhys fought to untangle his jeans from his leg and then get redressed.

"There," he said, stomping his shoes back on. "Now that I look mostly presentable again, how about if I take you to dinner before you and your skinny self waste away?"

"Skinny! I am not. I'm trim and fit, not scrawny. Thank you very much. Of course," he added and smirked, "a few more times like that, and I won't need my gym membership anymore."

"Ass," Rhys rumbled and slung his arm around Chase's shoulders. "We can take my bike and go for a ride after dinner."

Chase nodded, scared a little. How the man had gotten to him so deeply, he had no idea. But the only person in his life outside blood relations who knew more about him was James. He knew he should hate this, especially because it happened so fast, but instead all he felt was relief. "That sounds like a plan."

WHEN THEY exited, Rhys stopped short at the sight of a sticky note on his office door. He pulled it off and read it, then looked to where Mark's office door was closed. *Cheeky bastard,* he thought fondly, thankful their friendship was stronger than titanium, or he was certain Mark would have interrupted and killed him.

He handed the note to Chase and failed to stifle his amusement when Chase blushed and ducked his head. "Oh God. And I'm supposed to teach him and Aurora how to make those truffles her parents love," he whined.

"I'm sure you've been heard before."

"Yeah, but not by my *straight* friend and boss!"

"All it says is lock up and not to scare the neighbors too much. You'll be fine. Let's slip out, though, before he catches us and makes a liar out of me." He guided Chase outside, taking a moment to lock up before they went to dinner.

"STILL THINK you're being weird," Chase muttered and stomped into the living room at Rhys's place. "I'm perfectly capable of staying in my own apartment."

"I'm not leaving you alone yet, and that's final." Rhys tugged him down into his lap and wrapped his arms around him. "Not after this morning, cariadon."

Yeah, he didn't want to think about that morning. Truthfully, he didn't enjoy the idea of sleeping alone that night either, worried his old nightmares would return and he would end up screaming himself awake. Not that he wanted Rhys to see how broken that event had left him. "Just for tonight, though. I'm not some charity case. Okay?"

"No, you're my boyfriend, and as such, I get the right to be there for you when bad things happen."

"I'm not some helpless girl, ya know."

"Thank heaven for that. I don't do chicks!" Rhys laughed so hard he snorted, while Chase glowered. "Ah, come on. Even the hardest badass out there needs a friend once in a while."

"Fine, just remember who wears the pants in this family," Chase quipped, snuggling into Rhys more. He was so tired.

"Um, last time I checked, we both do, cariadon."

"Not the point," he mumbled and then thought about what Rhys had said. He'd called him that weird word again. More than a couple of times now, he thought. "Why do you keep calling me cari… that word?"

"I told you what it means. It's what my dad calls my mom, what Ryan called Janet, and what I intend to call you."

"It's not that I object to pet names, obviously, but I've never heard the word before you called me that back at the B&B."

Rhys shrugged, shifting his big body and Chase with the movement. "It just is, okay?" he grumbled.

Chase wasn't sure if Rhys was uncomfortable expressing why it was so important to him or if he thought Chase actually objected to the name. "It's nice, Rhys. Now, sit still so I can rest. You keep moving."

"Yes, dear." Rhys twisted once more before holding Chase against him and stroking his hair gently. Moments later, he remembered nothing, exhaustion having finally won.

chapter seventeen

CHASE WAS unsure how it happened, but the next week and a half flew by. He spent most nights with Rhys, usually in his loft above the office. Most days he spent focused on his consulting work and helping Mark and Rhys with anything not related to the murder-suicide cases. Grayson tended to those needs. Grayson was a quiet guy most of the time, but he was also very good at his work and loyal to Rhys above all else. Of course, Chase still wondered how the man was able to simply drop his life and leave DC on a moment's notice, but no one had answered that question yet.

"Hey, Chase, come on," Grayson said, interrupting his musings. "Rhys has been by three times now wanting to take you to lunch. The code will still be waiting for you when you get back."

He pivoted in his chair to face Grayson, confused as to what he was talking about. He didn't remember Rhys stopping by. "Huh?" he asked, rubbing his tired eyes.

"You are still dating the big, burly ginger boy, right? Him," he added and pointed to where Rhys stood speaking to Nichelle at the front desk. "He keeps coming by, but you ignore him every time."

I did? "I did not." He would remember that, right?

"You did. It's two thirty already, and you haven't moved from that spot in at least four hours. Even I can't stare at code that long without a break. Now, go on. I'll hold down the fort," he added, the edge of his lips turning up slightly. Chase had only seen Grayson really smile when joking around with Rhys, but he didn't feel he could pry into the man's life... yet.

"Two?"

"Thirty," Grayson added with a nod. "Now, shoo. Your stomach is loud enough to wake the dead."

Heat spread up his face at the comment. Now that he thought about it, yeah, he was hungry. Really hungry. "Think I will. Thanks."

He stood and stretched, only then realizing how stiff he was. He saved everything he was working on and closed down his programs before locking his computer. Chase grabbed his pack and then started toward the front reception area. However, his cell ringing interrupted him.

"Mom?" He didn't need to look at the display; it only rang "Für Elise" for his mother.

"Hi, sweetie. How's my favorite son?" Her voice was just as strong and smoky as always.

He smiled, thrilled to still have her in his life. "Hey, Mom. What's up?"

"Checking up on you, dear. What else?" She giggled. God, he loved his family. "Well, and wondering if I'm ever going to meet this mystery man I hear you're dating."

"Who tattled?" He was surprised she was only just now asking, honestly. He wasn't in the habit of keeping her on the outside of his relationships if they were serious, but him being with Rhys was something so different. He hadn't told her they were seeing each other.

"That nice friend of yours, James. I ran into him at the grocery store. He said you are seeing some detective.... Reece, maybe?"

"Rhys is a PI, not a detective, but yeah, I am. It's pretty new, though, so I hadn't introduced him to you yet."

"By the tone you're taking, I'm thinking he's important to you, so I want to meet him. Soon." Damn, he knew that attitude. That was pure Mama 101: Now Or Else.

"Yes, ma'am," he grumbled. Arms wrapped around him, and he caught the scent of Rhys. His man didn't wear cologne like he did, but he always seemed to smell fresh yet all man anyway. "I'll see when he's willing to stop by. But, uh, why aren't you at work?"

"Chase," she chided. "You know I only work a half day on Fridays."

"Oh, right." *It's Friday already? How had that happened?* "Well, I'm going to grab something to eat and get back to work. Promise I'll call you tonight, and we can set up a luncheon for you to meet him. 'Kay?"

132

"Sure, sweetie. Love you."

"Love you too." Chase clicked the end button and leaned back into Rhys's soothing embrace.

"Mm," Rhys rumbled against his ear. "I do love a man that loves his mama."

"Are you making fun of me?"

"No, sir. But how you relate to her tells me a lot about you. Now, are you finally ready for food?"

"Yeah. Grayson threw me out of my own office." Chase turned in Rhys's arms and pouted. "How does that even work?"

"He's a good man. Now, upstairs or out?"

"Upstairs is fine. I've got too much work still to do to be gone long. Well, unless I want to work all weekend too. Which I do not," he added before tugging Rhys up to his apartment.

"Plans this weekend?" Rhys asked, his voice devoid of emotion.

"Nothing major, just spend time with friends, you, avoid my parents…."

Rhys laughed, shaking his head, as he entered the kitchen. "The usual."

Chase riffled through the fridge before pulling out the roast beef, turkey, and ham slices. He then grabbed the Swiss cheese, hot mustard, mayonnaise, and toppings they preferred.

He set all the stuff for their sandwiches on the counter, then turned and closed the fridge. He grabbed the fresh bread he'd made the night before. Rhys grunted, opening the fridge to pull out sodas and some fruit as he set about his task. He sliced the bread thick before he put on the mustard and mayo. Chase looked over to Rhys, shrugged, and sliced both onion and tomato. When Rhys smirked, brow raised, he grinned. "What, you won't notice the onion on my breath, since yours will be just as bad."

"True. I was more impressed with the size of what you're building than which toppings, actually. I mean, you sure you're going to be able to wrap your mouth around that thing?"

"I can wrap my lips around anything I set my mind to, baby. And I do mean *anything*."

"Don't do that! Please, sweetheart, I have to go to an appointment when we're done, and I really do *not* need a hard-on for it."

"Mm… true, plus I don't want you flaunting what you've got where I can't partake." He laughed when Rhys groaned, sounding like he was in pain at the thought. *Good!*

He set their plates on the counter and sat beside Rhys. He didn't intend to take long for lunch but did want to spend the time with Rhys, so he refrained from hurrying back down with his food.

"By the way," he mumbled around his first bite, too hungry to wait or remember his manners. "Thanks for siccing Grayson on me."

"I didn't, but glad he got you to take a break. How are things coming, by the way?"

Chase swallowed hard and took a quick sip of the Coke Rhys gave him; he preferred Mountain Dew, but hadn't bought more since running out two days ago. "I finished the financial research Mark asked for and e-mailed it to him. I dropped a portable drive off for you with a copy of the rebuilt data from the desktop you brought me last night." He paused, thinking through his assigned work, trying to remember if there was something specific Rhys was still waiting on. "I have to finish the new website for Dale, and then I'll start searching through the phone and laptop from this morning."

"Dale?"

Chewing a huge bite of apple, he nodded and swallowed. "You know he has his own animal practice, right?" Rhys nodded, and he continued. "His vet tech, Lacy, tried to set one up for the clinic, but she doesn't have the skills needed to do all the back-end stuff he wants. He finally admitted defeat and called me," Chase explained and shrugged. He thought Dale should have come to him in the first place, but as flighty and playful as Dale could be, his pride was often his biggest issue.

"It's nice of you to help him out." Rhys took his last bite of food, washing it down with his Coke. "Just don't let your friends bog down your workload."

Chase stopped midchew and stared at Rhys. Was he jealous, or did he really think Chase's friends would try to take advantage of him? "They don't, hun, and I don't think I like what you're implying. Dale is a paying customer, who happens to be my friend. I did offer him a discount, but he refused, insisting he should pay what my work is worth. I know you don't really know him yet, but he's a good guy, if a little too much of a party boy at times."

"Party boy? Thought you liked being a party boy too?"

"I go out with friends and dance, drink some, and have fun, but I don't take home tricks. Never have."

Rhys raised his brows, and the pinched set of his lips worried Chase. He knew his appearance was a sore point but didn't know it would bother Rhys to know Dale was a bit of a slut at times. His friend was always careful and got tested religiously, so Chase never thought much of it. "What diff does it make to you how Dale acts when he goes out? He's loyal, loving, and a sweetheart. What more could you want in a friend?"

"One that's faithful," Rhys mumbled, not meeting Chase's eyes.

"Rhys?"

"Don't want you out with your friends and have them try to convince you it's cool to go home with someone else."

Chase counted to ten in his head three times before deciding he was calm enough to speak. He hoped. "One, I said loyal. That includes to a partner if he's dating someone, you ass. Two, since when do I let others make choices about my life or body?" he asked, making sure his tone was as sour as he felt. "And three, he's not *your* boyfriend, so what does it matter to you?"

"I just—Guess it shouldn't. I just don't like the idea of it, is all."

"You don't have to like it. But I *do* like him, so you are going to have to get over it."

"Fine," he mumbled, not looking at Chase.

"I know exactly what we need to do tomorrow night," Chase said, ignoring Rhys's sulking.

"Hm? What's that?"

"Simon and Dale invited me to go clubbing with them. You'll come with us."

"So I can watch a bunch of horny guys slobber all over you? I don't think so."

Oh, this was going to be fun! "Please, baby," Chase begged. He turned and slipped from his seat to straddle Rhys's lap. "Our dance at the

135

club before was fun, right?" He rubbed his half-hard cock against Rhys's tight abs. "You *sure* you don't want to come with us?"

"Oh God. Keep that up, and you won't make it back to work today."

"Ooh, afternoon delight? My fave," Chase cooed. He moved the chair enough so he could slip between Rhys's legs and down on his knees.

Rubbing the heel of his hand against Rhys's cock seemed to rob the man of all speech. Rhys watched him massage his thighs. Chase unbuckled the belt and unzipped his jeans, relishing how the bulge grew and Rhys's breathing sped up.

He grabbed Rhys's legs and pulled, sliding him down until his thighs were on both sides of Chase. As soon as he peeled down the boxers, he noticed how damp they were over the tip and smiled. He flicked out his tongue, catching the bead of precome sitting in the slit. Rhys gasped and arched, but Chase held his hips down.

"Not yet," he whispered, reveling in the taste and scent of his man. Taking his time, he licked under the edge of the foreskin, teasing and nibbling as he did. He wrapped his right hand around Rhys's throbbing member, squeezing lightly.

"Please," Rhys breathed, his eyes riveted on Chase.

Chase loved what he was doing—making a man like this whimper and writhe with nothing more than his hands and mouth. Giving himself over to Rhys's pleasure, he dived on Rhys's cock, swallowing it, pulling it all the way to the back of his throat as he laved and hummed, sending shock waves through his prey.

Rhys's breath came faster, in gasps and moans, his hips rocking forward. His fingers tangled in Chase's hair. Chase sped his pace, sucking harder and dropping his other hand to tug and massage Rhys's balls. After a few more seconds, Rhys groaned, his fingers tightening to the point of pain as he yielded his load. Chase gulped repeatedly, determined not to spill a drop of his lover's essence.

He waited as Rhys's breathing calmed and his fingers finally released the death grip on Chase's hair, loving how blissed out his lover was. When Rhys opened his eyes, Chase smiled up at him. "Feel better, baby?"

"Uh-huh. Give me a minute to restart my brain, and I'll return the favor."

Chase sat back on his heels. He knew he was frowning, but couldn't help it. "This isn't a tit-for-tat kind of thing." He stood smoothly and stepped to the side, adjusting himself. He started cleaning up from lunch, unsure how to address how Rhys's words made him feel.

"Chase?" Rhys said behind him.

"Hm?" He didn't stop, though he was painfully aware of how close Rhys stood behind him. "I'll be done in a minute, hun, and we can go back to work."

"Chase, stop." Rhys's voice was strong, as were the hands that took hold of his shoulders, halting him in mid wipe down. "I didn't mean it like that, sweetheart."

He cocked his head, listening but not turning yet. He couldn't explain to himself why he was upset, so how could he make Rhys understand?

"I wanted to return the pleasure, make you feel good. I wasn't trying to upset you."

"I know that. I do, I just…." He shrugged, at a total loss for words.

"Someone treated you that way, huh?"

He cringed, hating how easily Rhys could read him. He shrugged, hoping Rhys wouldn't push.

"Chase, talk to me." It was an order, not a request.

"It's not important. Really," he added and turned, wrapping his arms around Rhys's waist. "I'm being stupid." He didn't want to discuss how crappy his relationship with Jonathan had been or why he'd left the ass. Hell, it had been years since he'd even seen Jon, so he was pissed at himself for letting old pains still hurt him.

Rhys sighed but hugged Chase back. "One day soon you are going to have to start opening up some."

Chase shifted back and pulled on his cuff, knowing Rhys was right. He still hadn't told him about his exes, his family, or let Rhys see his scars. He knew Rhys knew about what had happened, how his uncle had almost killed them both instead of only Ethan, but he still feared Rhys's reaction. "I'll try," he mumbled, frustrated by how a blowjob had turned into *this*.

Instead of responding as Chase had expected him to, Rhys took hold of his left hand and raised it to his lips. "You," he whispered across

Chase's knuckles. "Are an amazing." He flipped Chase's hand and kissed his palm. "Strong," he continued, and slipped the first buckle on the cuff loose. "Man, that I'm," he murmured and unhooked the other thin buckle. "Honored to know. And nothing in your past will change that." Rhys slipped the leather piece off his wrist and looked down at the only truly ugly place on his body.

"I know, nasty," Chase choked out, hating the scar almost as much as he hated that he'd done that to himself. Chase expected revulsion or at least the Rhys patented scowl. What he got instead made his head spin and his heart hurt.

"It's a battle scar, same as any on me," Rhys countered. Instead of pulling back, he leaned down and teased the twisted flesh with the tip of his tongue.

Chase gasped, then moaned. No one had ever touched him there. He never imagined someone would want to. "You don't have to do…. Oh God, Rhys. Why are you—"

"Why am I doing this?" Rhys asked, then teased his wrist again with tongue and lips. "Because all of you is worthy of attention and love, sweetheart."

His eyes prickled, but he fought back the tears. How could Rhys be so…. He wasn't even certain what Rhys was being, but it boggled his mind. "Can we…. Will you…."

"What, Chase? What do you need?" Instead of waiting for an answer, Rhys scooped him up and headed to the bedroom. He settled down on the bed, but instead of getting friendly like he normally would, Rhys draped Chase over his body, holding his damaged wrist and rubbing his thumb over the sensitive skin that was normally never exposed.

He wanted to fight the strange actions of his lover, but instead he found himself dozing off, reality fading until even the steady thumping of Rhys's heart beneath his ear lulled him, and soon, sleep took him completely.

chapter eighteen

CHASE WAS at his huge computer desk working on an interactive customer system for one of his clients when his attention was drawn away from the monitor and specs sheet by arguing. Sometimes clients got loud when Rhys or Mark gave them bad news, like a husband receiving proof his devoted wife wasn't so devoted, but this sounded different. Besides, it was still early, and he didn't remember Rhys having any client meetings that morning.

He saved and locked the computer, and then he stepped away to find out what was going on. Before he made it past the doorway, Grayson was right on his heels. When he looked out, he noted Rhys was following—or maybe chasing—a short, stocky cop toward the IT area.

"Step just outside the tech area, but don't get too far," Grayson whispered.

Chase turned enough to see the man out of the corner of his eye. "What's going on?" he asked just as softly.

"Don't know, but Rhys is pissed, and I'm not moving from your side until things calm down."

Chase was certain Grayson meant the words to soothe, but instead they made him more concerned about why a cop was storming his way. Deciding to go for friendly instead of scared or hostile, he put on his best face and smiled. "Hello, Officer."

The cop stopped abruptly in front of him, looked him up and down once, and sneered. "You Chase Manning?"

"Yep, that's me. How can I help you?" Chase saw Rhys tense and his mouth open, but he cut him off before he could lay into the guy. "Rhys, shush."

He reached out and snagged Rhys's arm, pulling him to stand on his other side, effectively placing Rhys and Grayson as his guards.

If anything, the sneer turned into a full-on scowl of revulsion. "Ruiz. Officer Ruiz. Think you can remember that?"

Chase blinked a few times, irritated with the hostility and the disgust dripping from the man's words. "Sure. Now, how 'bout you tell me what it is you need from me so you can hurry up and leave, since you so obviously don't want to be here."

"Damn freaks," Ruiz muttered before pulling out a notepad and looking it over.

Rhys tensed again, but Chase tightened his grip, hoping he could control things instead of Rhys ending up in jail. He had no idea what had already been said, but Rhys seemed ready to kill.

"Did you know a Randall Tyler?"

Did, not do? "I know Randy. Haven't seen him in probably close to two years. Why?" *What the hell is going on?*

"Thought so. Seems another of your pervy exes slipped on a blade and died. Don't suppose you...."

He was certain the man kept talking, but he couldn't make out the words. All he could hear was the sudden roaring in his ears as he flashed back to the day he'd run into his cousin's room, then into his bathroom, and found his best friend and closest thing to a brother—twin, practically—any kid could have in the tub full of red water. Any thoughts after that were too muddled to process.

Rhys's rage-filled scream tore him from his breakdown. It still took him a moment to figure out what the hell was going on. Mark and Grayson each had one of Rhys's arms as he struggled against their hold, screaming at the cop.

"I'll have your damn badge, you homophobic piece of shit. Get off my property and stay away from Chase!"

The two men continued to throw insults, both red-faced and screaming when the reality of what was happening finally hit Chase. Shaking so hard he could barely walk, he threw himself against Rhys's back, wrapping his arms around him. He pressed close, making sure Rhys could feel all of him. "Rhys, stop it. Now."

Rhys stilled and went quiet, though Chase could feel him trembling with barely restrained violence. Chase turned his head toward Mark, not shifting even a millimeter from his irate boyfriend. He struggled to ignore both his memories and the cop's venomous words. "Mark, please escort the officer out, and then call whoever you need to to report his actions."

"I'm here to question you!" Ruiz snapped, clutching his service weapon. Chase was thankful to see the strap was still secure.

"I will come down to the station with my lawyer and answer any legitimate questions asked of me. For now, though, leave or deal with the consequences."

"How dare you threaten me," Ruiz growled. He took a step forward, which was all that was needed for Rhys to lunge for the man. If it weren't for the hold all three of them had on Rhys, he would have connected, Chase was certain.

Moments later, two cops came in the front door and dragged Ruiz out with them. They both apologized but left quickly. It took a good half hour for Chase to piece it all together, most of which Rhys spent pacing and growling at anyone who got near him. Randall Tyler, or Randy as his friends called him, had been found in his apartment, wrists slashed, early that morning. There had been signs of obsession all over his room. Things such as dozens and dozens of photos of Chase taken with telescopic lenses and candles surrounding a photo of Chase. And just like with Mike, Randy was one of his exes. But he couldn't believe the possessive markers he learned of—that wasn't Randy's style. Besides, they had ended as friends, though not close ones.

His work forgotten, he sat in the reception area, watching Rhys and pondering what to do. "Rhys? What are we missing? Why can't anyone figure out who's doing this?"

Rhys stopped and faced him, finally seeming to see him again. "I don't know. There's no trace of whoever this psycho is, or if there is, the police aren't sharing that info with us."

"There wasn't anything in any of the stuff you brought in either," Grayson added as he came over to where he sat. "I get how the police might miss something, but I don't understand how the killer's staying ahead of Rhys and Mark. But, uh…." he trailed off, looking away from Chase suddenly.

"But what?" Rhys snapped, turning toward Grayson.

Grayson shifted from foot to foot, staring down. After a moment, he raised his gaze to meet Chase's. "You might think about tracking down any other exes still living in the area." His eyes flicked to Rhys and back. "Not like tricks or anything, but this is your second ex the killers have taken out. Others from your past may be in danger as well."

Since he'd snapped out of his memories earlier, Chase had managed to ignore implications and fears such as those. Now, however, it all came crashing down on him again, and before he knew it, the world got dark around the edges, and Rhys was kneeling beside him, rubbing his back and demanding he breathe.

"Come on, breathe, sweetheart. You're safe. I won't let anyone hurt you, promise."

"As do I," Mark said the same time as Grayson said, "Agreed."

Chase sat back in the chair, fighting to get control of his fears and feelings, not something he usually had so much trouble doing. "I know you won't, none of you. My head gets it, really, even if the rest of me forgets sometimes. Sorry for being such a wuss," he mumbled, mortified he'd fallen apart again.

"You're not," Rhys countered. "But Grayson's right. Any other exes in the area still might be in danger. They need to be warned."

Chase nodded, looking around. His eyes landed on Nichelle as she peeked over her desk, chewing her bottom lip. "Nikki, you okay?" he asked.

She nodded with quick, jerky movements. "Just scared for you, that's all. Oh, and Rhys, 911 has most of what that ass said to you and Chase, so…." She paused and wiped her eyes with a tissue. "Call your lawyer friend, Mr. Holcomb, and isn't your dad friends with that idiot's captain? I recognized him. He works with Dal."

Rhys's worried face morphed to one of evil glee in the blink of an eye. "He does?" When she nodded, he grinned.

"And how do they have a recording?" Mark asked.

"'Cause I called 911 and stayed on the phone with them the entire time. So, you," she said, looking at Rhys, "nail his ass." She then turned to

Chase. "And you, do you need help finding anyone? I'll help you look up numbers and such if you want."

Twenty minutes later, Rhys was in his office making calls, Grayson was hard at work behind Chase, and Chase was staring at the phone number and address of his only other still local ex. God, he did not want to talk to Jonathan. Ever. Nevertheless, he knew leaving the man clueless was wrong and stupid, especially since he'd heard Jonathan had a family. He also knew trying to call would be pointless. As soon as Jonathan figured out who it was, he would hang up and either not answer again or block his calls.

It had been a few weeks between each death, though it didn't seem like it with how time passed since he and Rhys had become a couple. He decided he wasn't ready for the confrontation yet, though. Instead, he spent part of the afternoon talking on the phone to James about everything. He hated to burden his BFF, but Jamie was the only person he could tell all this to who would understand and not judge or try to "fix it" for him.

He'd only just hung up with James when Rhys appeared in the doorway, a deep frown marring his handsome, chiseled face. "Chase?"

"What's up, hun?" He was annoyed at how flat his voice was, knowing it would make Rhys worry, but unable to make himself sound more normal.

"Just got off the phone with Dal, and he needs you to come down for a formal interview. Carter—his captain and a friend of our dad's—decided since you and Dal are friends, he'd make Dal the liaison for this meeting."

"Okay. That is what we told them to do, so it shouldn't surprise you. But hey, the guys in charge of Dal's precinct were good to James, so I see no reason to think the ass hat from earlier is indicative of how I'll be treated."

"Naw, Carter won't let that happen. Besides, I already called Mel Holcomb, Seth's lawyer, and he'll meet us there."

"Yes, hun, I know who Mel is," Chase teased gently. "Thanks for calling him. This is all so crazy."

"I know, but I'm not willing to risk anything more happening, so I'll drive you over and wait. Dal will be there too, so you'll be safe."

Chase looked Rhys over, perplexed by the way his lover fidgeted. He was hiding something. "What aren't you saying, Rhys?"

"Too observant for your own good." Chase stared, hoping Rhys would spill. "Fine. Two things. One, at least for right now, I would really like it if you stayed here with me. Or if you don't want to deal with me that much, stay with one of your friends or Mark. I don't want you home alone."

He thought about it and had to agree. He didn't like the idea of being alone either, not that he would admit that. He kinda liked the idea of staying with Rhys. See if they could stand each other when put together that long. "All right," he agreed but then added, "for now. What else?"

"My dad called earlier," Rhys said, then paused. Chase rolled his hand, motioning him to continue. "He wants us to come over for lunch tomorrow."

"I didn't know you'd told your parents about us yet, but okay. Why the panic?"

Rhys scuffed the toe of his boot on the carpet before looking up. "You've put your mom off about meeting me for a week now, I wasn't sure you'd want to go."

Chase shook his head, frustrated with his brilliant twit of a lover. "Rhys, I've asked you three times when you want to meet her, but you change the subject every time. I thought *you* weren't ready to be that involved. You know, like it's too soon for you, or something."

Rhys stared at him, mouth ajar. "I…. You…. What?"

"What, what? I didn't want to push you if you weren't ready."

The loud, rumbling laugh Rhys let out startled him but had him chuckling along moments later. "We're both idiots, ya know. Fine, I'll meet yours and you can meet mine. I'll call Mom on the way to the interview and find out when. 'Kay?"

Nodding, Rhys smiled down at him. "Sounds good."

THREE HOURS later, Chase was certain God hated him. He knew someone did, at the very least. Stuck in the small, annoyingly bright room with a couple of cops and their captain was not his idea of fun. He was thankful for Mel's presence, though he hadn't needed a lawyer for anything other than show. They had stayed on point and not tried playing the word games he knew cops often used to pull more information out of a person than they wanted to give. But in this case, he honestly did not know anything to help them. He gave them the list of his exes, but he didn't see that helping either.

Once the meeting was finally over, he stood outside with Red, Dal's police partner, while Dal and Rhys spoke a few feet away. The entire day had been horrible, and looking at the concerned frowns on the brothers' faces wasn't making him any less nervous.

"It'll be okay, man. Rhys is good at his job, and if anyone can protect you until we can catch this bastard, it's him," Red said.

"I know he can. I'm not worried about that. I'm scared this psycho might go after him too." It was the first time he'd actually said the words aloud, and he cringed at the thought. He was torn up enough over seeming to be the focus of a serial killer, but he couldn't stand the thought of losing Rhys.

"Hey," Red said, bumping his shoulder. "Dude's an ex-Marine. He was the baddest of the bad, ya know. I'd be more worried for the perp than for Rhys if he gets his hands on the guy. We'll need a body bag, not handcuffs, for anyone stupid enough to take on him or his brother."

Chase knew his smile was faint, but Red's confidence in Rhys helped calm him, though nothing would be right until this was all over. "Thanks."

"Just truth, man. Come on, they look like they're wrapping things up, and you look like you need some serious sleep." Red led him over to where the Sayer brothers still spoke.

"Thanks for being here tonight," Rhys said to Dal as they reached him.

Chase leaned into Rhys's side as Rhys wrapped one bulging arm around his shoulders. "Can we go?" he asked softly, no longer having the energy to pretend things were okay.

"Of course, cariadon."

Dal looked at Rhys, inhaling sharply, but didn't say anything. Chase wondered what that was about, but figured he could ask later. Right then, he just wanted to go back to Rhys's and sleep, preferably with Rhys curled around him. "Thanks," he murmured as Rhys said his good-byes and led him back to the car.

chapter nineteen

CHASE STOOD outside the rambling ranch-style house of his ex, trying to bolster his courage and approach the door. Why Jonathan still had the power this many years later to affect him like this was beyond him. Sadly, that didn't change the fact he was still terrified of how Jonathan would react to him appearing on his doorstep like this. Much less to what Chase was there to tell him.

Last he'd heard, Jonathan had married some woman and had, he thought, two children. He was still at a loss as to why Jonathan had been the way he was at the end of their relationship. The fighting and insults were bad enough, but to run into the arms of some unsuspecting woman and lie to everyone was beyond stupid in his book. Not that anyone had asked him.

After standing there for a few more minutes, Chase swallowed hard and approached the door. When he'd made it up the three steps, he raised his hand and knocked, wishing Jonathan would and would not answer. For good or ill, the door opened, and there before him was his ex. The man stared at him, not saying a word as he looked Chase up and down. The look on his face told Chase louder than any words could that his presence was not welcome.

Tough shit, he thought. "Hi, Jonathan," he said but paused when Jonathan grasped him by his right wrist hard enough to hurt. He was suddenly yanked inside and the door closed.

"What the hell are you doing here, Chase?" Jonathan asked, his voice like ice.

When he didn't answer fast enough, the grip on his wrist tightened and twisted until he had trouble staying standing. Jonathan pushed him back against the wall and the man Chase had once thought loved him sneered, their noses almost touching. "I asked you a question, you sick fuck. What are you doing here? I don't want anyone to think I'd actually hang out with someone like you!"

"I… I came to warn you about a possible threat. I'm trying to protect you, not mess up your Rockwell painting of a life." Dammit! Why was he back to being that scared and empty teen again? He knew how to defend himself.

"You? You're warning me off what? I don't swing that way, boy! And I don't want anything you have."

Chase fought not to struggle, knowing it would only make Jonathan angrier. The last time they'd had words, he had limped away with two cracked ribs and a ton of bruises. He should have taken Rhys up on his offer to come with him, but Chase had been afraid it would turn into a pissing match, if not a brawl, between the mistake of his past and the hope of a future. Besides, he never wanted Jonathan to know of Rhys, much less be near the man he loved.

He struggled for a deep breath, hating the feeling of being pinned and of how much his chest and wrist were hurting already. "Someone killed Mike and Randy. The cops investigating say someone's been going after my exes to get to me, though no one knows why," he explained, forcing as much calm into his voice as possible. "I wanted to warn you so you would be able to protect your family. I don't want anyone hurt."

"How dare you speak of my family!" Jonathan roared. "You don't get to even think of them, much less anything else. I don't want them tainted with the likes of you."

"Let me go, Jonathan," Chase demanded. He yelped when, instead of releasing him, Jonathan twisted harder. White-hot pain shot up his arm and down his fingers. Still reeling from that, he was blindsided when Jonathan pulled his arm back and delivered a powerful jab to his ribs.

Instead of taking it like he always had before, Chase lashed out instinctively, unable to see clearly through the stinging tears the brutal handling and hit caused. "Don't you ever touch me again!" he screamed as he started hitting and kicking, catching Jonathan solidly in the groin.

Jonathan went to his knees, yowling in pain. "Don't give a damn if the psycho gets you. Wouldn't have even come if I didn't care about innocent people getting hurt," he continued yelling. He kicked one last time, clipping Jonathan in the shoulder and sending him tumbling backward.

Moments later Chase was outside, gulping the fresh air. He sprinted to his car, not wanting to give Jonathan the chance to catch him again. He made it all of two blocks before the shaking forced him to pull over and stop the car.

He sat there, trying to get hold of himself, cradling his wrist to his chest until the trembling stopped and he was able to think again. "What the hell was I thinking? Should have let the cops notify him."

He jumped when his cell rang. That small sound had him trembling again. He managed to get his cell out of his pocket, though it hurt like hell to use his right hand and wrist even that much.

"Hello?"

"Chase? What's wrong?" Rhys asked, his voice low.

"N-nothing. I'll tell you later. What's up?"

"You're supposed to meet me at Mom and Dad's, remember? I was going to ask you to stop and get us something to bring, but now I'm thinking I should cancel and come to wherever you are."

"No, no. That's not necessary," he countered, needing a few more minutes to collect himself. "I'll be there in a little bit, and do you seriously think I didn't get something for your mom? Meeting your parents for the first time with no hostess gift? Yeah, Mom would kill me."

Rhys laughed, helping to calm Chase more. He told Rhys he'd be there in a few, then clicked off. He checked his wrist, not amused by the bruising and puffiness. Instead of driving right over, he stopped by his place to change into a long-sleeved top, intent on hiding how his wrist looked. He knew he couldn't hide it for long, but hoped it wasn't as bad as he feared.

By the time he made it to the elder Sayer residence, he was calm, dressed sharply, and thanks to some Aleve, mostly pain-free. Rhys was at his side almost before he had the bike stopped. He had switched to the bike as planned, hoping Rhys would take that to mean he really was okay. He hadn't gotten the key out of the ignition before Rhys's huge hand cupped his face carefully.

"Sweetheart? You okay?" Rhys asked, looking Chase over carefully.

"Yeah. You want to step back so I can get off my bike?"

"Oh, sure." Rhys stepped back, but only enough for him to dismount. As soon as Chase was standing, though, Rhys was running his hands all over him.

Chase was resolved about not showing any discomfort to Rhys until his lover grabbed his hand and tugged lightly. "Agh!" Chase barked, the pain overriding his intentions.

"What?" Rhys snapped. He brought Chase's hand up, carefully this time, and inspected the damage. He had Chase's sleeve unbuttoned and up to his elbow in seconds and stared down at the already discoloring flesh.

"It's fine, Rhys. We're here to meet with your parents, so let's go in." He didn't wait for Rhys to respond. He fixed his sleeve before grabbing the bottle of wine and small bouquet of flowers from the pack on the back of his bike.

"No, it's not, Chase. Did that Jonathan guy do this to you?"

"Drop it," Chase begged. He already felt bad enough. He didn't need Rhys freaking out too. "We can discuss it later. I would really rather not start things off with your parents thinking I'm some pathetic wimp, 'kay? Now, I don't see either of Dal's vehicles. Isn't he supposed to be here too?"

"Fine, but I want a look at that wrist, cariadon. And no, Dal's not here yet, but he will be."

Hoping to refocus his protective love, Chase inquired, "Is he bringing that guy he asked out?"

Rhys shook his head. "No, I asked, but he said something about it being too soon. I'm thinking it's more like he's afraid they won't approve instead of not being willing to introduce him, though."

"That doesn't sound like Dal," They entered the well-appointed home Rhys had grown up in. The foyer was huge and opened onto a large sitting area, but he didn't see anyone. "Um, aren't your mom and dad supposed to be here too?"

"They are, sweetheart. Dad's in his office, and Mom is in the kitchen. Let's drop these things off with her, and then I want to check your wrist better before lunch."

Chase sighed, annoyed that Rhys wouldn't let go of the issue but kind of enjoying the care and attention. He loved Rhys in protector mode. It was sexy as hell, usually. "But not where they can see, all right?"

"Fine."

Rhys led him through the dining room. Well, the formal one, he assumed by the huge table, chandelier, and dark wood tones. When he stepped into the next room, he was surprised to see the huge, bright kitchen. It was unlike the rest of the house so far, all stainless steel and granite and open. Very sleek and modern, while the rest of the house was staid and formal. Considering how informal Rhys and Dal were most of the time, the entire place didn't seem to fit.

"Hey, Mom," Rhys said as a beautiful older woman looked up from cutting vegetables at the center counter. She set down her knife, a huge smile blooming on her face. She had fine lines around her eyes, and her red hair was more silver than ginger, but it was easy to see she was related to the Sayer boys.

"Rhys!" she exclaimed, her accent enchanting him. He kind of wished Rhys carried a bit more of it in his speech. She hurried around the counter to wrap Rhys in a huge hug. The woman was so tiny in comparison to her eldest, it made Chase smile. She would be short even to him.

"Hey. Mom, I wanted you to meet someone very important to me." He pulled away from her and wrapped his arm about Chase's shoulders, pulling him closer. "This is Chase Manning."

Chase pasted on his best Mom smile and held out the flowers, Rhys having taken the wine before they came inside. "Hi, Mrs. Sayer. Your home is lovely."

"Oh, thank you, dear," she said, taking the flowers. "They're beautiful. Please, call me Elain, though. I mean, if you're going to be part of the family, we should be on first-name basis, right?"

Family? "Thank you, Elain."

"Oh, Chase brought you this too," Rhys added, holding out the merlot. "And I know you have a million questions, but I wanted to introduce Chase to Dad before Dal gets here and we sit down to eat."

"Oh, okay, dear. He's in his office," she explained, and Chase noted a sour tone to her voice and her lips pursed slightly. He would have to ask

Rhys what that was about later. "Lunch will be ready in about fifteen. I hope your brother gets here in time. I hate starting late."

"I know, Mom. He'll be here soon, and we will be right back."

"Good." She kissed him on the cheek when he bent down, then returned to her food preparations as they headed back into the main part of the house.

"She seems really nice, Rhys."

"Yeah, but something's bugging her, not that she'll tell what it is until she's good and ready. Come on." Rhys led him down a hall and stopped at a plain door. He opened it and flipped on a light, revealing the room to be a largish half-bath.

"We are not making out in here," Chase teased, knowing they were in there because of his injury, not Rhys's insatiable passion—though he was rather insatiable most of the time.

RHYS SIGHED at Chase's attempt to lighten things. He was worried, and Chase making jokes wasn't helping his mood. He closed the door, then turned to face his love. "Don't make light of this, cariadon. Someone hurt you. I have every right to check the damage."

Chase looked away, eyes down as he presented his arm. "I'm sorry, hun. I didn't want to stress you, is all. Really, I'll be fine."

He took Chase's arm, careful of his wrist, and again unbuttoned and moved the sleeve out of his way. There were clear lines of bruising he was certain matched Chase's ex's fingers. Rhys closed his eyes, fighting his desire to go kill the man who thought it okay to treat *his* Chase in such a manner.

When he opened his eyes again, he raised the wrist and gently brushed his lips across the skin. "I'm so sorry you were hurt. Did he injure you anywhere else?"

"I think in the end I probably did more damage to him than he to me. He's probably icing his balls right now," he explained, and snickered.

"Good, but I want you to report this."

Even before he'd finished speaking, Chase was already shaking his head. "No. It's done and over with. Jonathan won't come after me. He was just upset because he's that deeply in denial of who he is. My being there was a threat to his safe little house of cards."

"I don't care what his reason was. Hurting you is not acceptable."

"I said no. It's my call, and I won't make it. Now, don't you have a dad to speak to and a brother to find?"

Rhys ground his teeth, pissed Chase seemed to be blowing off such an attack. "Chase...."

"No, and that's final. Let's go see who we can find, huh?"

He counted to twenty in his head, slowly, before he spoke again, knowing nothing short of a miracle would get Chase to listen. "Fine, but we will discuss this more later."

"I know, hun. I know."

They made it as far as the foyer when he heard Dal pull up outside. He decided a detour was in order. He had spoken to his father before Chase arrived and wasn't in any great hurry to rush back. His father was in a strange mood, one Rhys didn't know how to interpret and felt uncomfortable around.

He opened the door as Dal pulled up the drive.

"What're you grinning at?" he called once Dal had lined up his Ducati with their bikes and cut the engine.

"Chase," he said, nodding to the bright metallic-blue Sabre beside Rhys's Softail. Dal squinted as he stared at Chase.

"It's not what it looks like," Chase said defensively and turned away slightly before stepping around Rhys. He smiled at Dal, though Rhys noticed how shaky it seemed.

Dal stopped in front of Chase, frowning hard as he continued to look him over. Rhys knew what Dal would notice, how Chase's eyes were puffy and bloodshot and how his skin seemed a little paler than normal. He was just thankful his mother had been polite enough not to comment, knowing it would embarrass Chase if she fawned over him.

"What happened?" Dal demanded.

"Cool it, Dal. I'm sorry for scaring you," Chase said, not quite meeting his eyes. "It's just been a difficult few weeks, and I just came from talking to Jonathan."

"I don't know—"

"High school boyfriend," Chase snapped, cutting Dal off and spiking his worry again. "Seems he's back to being a 'good Christian boy,'" Chase explained, making air quotes. "He has a wife, coupla kids, and the whole white-picket-fence deal. He wasn't happy to see me, to say the least."

"Hey, his loss, right?" Dal murmured as he looked from Chase to Rhys and back.

"My good fortune," Rhys added, wrapping his arm around Chase's slender shoulders.

Chase smiled weakly as he looked up into Rhys's face. "Thanks for saying so."

"Hey, if he hadn't been so stupid as to give you up, I might have never gotten my chance."

"Pretending to be a battering ram was what got you your chance, not Jonathan's betra—" Chase stopped talking and tugged on his leather wrist cuff.

Dal took the lead and went inside, turning toward their dad's office, Chase behind him and Rhys following. Not that things were any more normal after that than before, though. Thanks to his lagging behind, Rhys came in partway through his father grousing about something or other.

"Now, where is your brother?" Bryn asked when they were still a step or two behind Dal.

"Right here, old man," he said from behind Dal and took Chase's hand in his.

"Don't get fresh, son." Bryn scowled. Chase shifted beside him, and while he loved his man being close, Rhys didn't appreciate his father upsetting Chase.

"Sorry, Dad."

Bryn nodded, his gaze zeroing in on Chase. "Seeing as both my sons seems to have lost their manners, hello. I'm Bryn Sayer."

"Chase, Chase Manning, sir. Nice to meet you."

A small smile flashed across Bryn's face as he looked Chase over. "Thank you. So, you're Rhys's new boy?"

Chase scrunched up his nose, opening his mouth before he snapped it closed again. Dal chuckled, as did Rhys. Chase hated being referred to that way, but he also knew Chase would try not to insult his father.

"What?" Bryn asked, his tone higher than before.

Chase squared his shoulders. "If anyone is anyone's *boy*, then it's Rhys who's *my* boy, not the other way around," Chase said succinctly, arms folded.

Bryn choked on a startled chuckle, and Dal lost all control of himself, laughing so hard he leaned over to brace his hands on his knees.

"Lunch is ready, boys," Elain said from the doorway.

"Yes, ma'am," Rhys and Dal said in unison.

"We'll be right there, cariadon," Bryn replied.

By the time they all calmed and made it to the dining room, Elain had the food served and directed each man to his seat.

"Thank you, Mrs. Sayer. This looks wonderful," Chase crooned over the meal.

She smiled brightly, sitting up a little straighter. "Eat, eat. You're going to have to work hard to keep up with the others."

As they ate, light conversation wafted about the table, no one discussing anything too heavy. At one point, Elain jumped into the conversation. "So, how long ago did you meet Chase, sweetie?"

Rhys looked up from his plate. "Almost a year ago, I think. It was right before Seth Burns hired me to protect his husband and daughter."

"So, this is a long courtship, then?" she asked.

"I sorta put your son through the ringer to prove he was serious before I agreed to date him," Chase said.

"As well you should, young man. Relationships are not something you should be frivolous about."

Conversation continued until his father was most of the way through his meal—eating was a priority, even to serious talk.

"So, are you dating anyone?" Bryn asked suddenly, staring at Dal hard.

Dal swallowed the bite he'd just taken, coughing as it went down wrong. "Um...."

"I think it's about time you settled down, Dal. Rhys seems to have done so. I hope." It wasn't a question or a statement. It was a demand.

"I have," Rhys replied to the order. "Not about to let Chase get away."

Chase shook his head, gripping Rhys's hand on the table where they could all see.

"I'm only twenty-eight, Dad."

"And your mom and I aren't getting any younger. It is high time you found a nice girl and had a baby or two. Your mother would so love to be a grandmother while we are still young enough to enjoy our grandchildren."

"But Dal's bi," Chase grumbled loud enough for everyone to hear. "What if he wants a husband instead of a wife?"

"Rhys may have a husband. He is gay and therefore cannot be in a real relationship with a woman. But Dal can be." Bryn paused and looked at Elain before continuing. "There is no reason Dal cannot have a normal relationship with a woman and uphold his family name and honor."

chapter twenty

RHYS PULLED up outside the GLBT teen center he and Dal were acting as security for that night and looked around. He didn't see Dal's bike but knew he would be there soon. What he didn't know was how Dal was doing, considering the insanity of their dad's demand. Giving his report on the cute little thing Dal was dating wasn't real high on his "want to do" list either, but he'd promised Dal a few days before that he would do a little digging and knew he couldn't hold off on sharing what he knew now any longer.

Shrugging, he went inside, hoping the dance would be incident-free. He wasn't even there for chaperoning, like most of the adults wandering around. No, he was there as a bouncer, to protect the kids attending the dance from any possible hate thrown their way.

After wandering around a little to scope out the best vantage points, he made his way over to the center's co-head, Cynthia Jazz. "Hey, Ms. Jazz."

"Oh, Rhys! How wonderful, so glad you could make it. Is that brother of yours here yet?" She smiled, showing off even, white teeth and distinguished laugh lines. She was older, but he hadn't dared ask how old. She was still very beautiful, if you went for women.

"No, ma'am, not yet. I just wanted to let you know he would be and that I was. We won't let anything happen that shouldn't."

"Such a good boy," she replied and patted his cheek. He found her amusing. Six months ago, she hadn't known who he was, yet now she treated him the same as some of his mom's friends did.

"Thanks." He flashed a smile but gazed around the room as she spoke. "I'll check in later with you, but I want to do a few things before the dance officially starts."

Ten minutes later, Dal approached. "Ready for tonight?"

Rhys looked up from his cell and grinned. "Always. You send a message to the club so someone tells Dad's tramp you won't be there?" He still couldn't believe their father had not only demanded Dal marry and have kids, but had gone so far as to set Dal up on a blind date with the daughter of some friend.

"Yeah." He sighed. "Sadly, I doubt this will deter him from trying again." Dal looked past Rhys, scanning the milling people.

"Your cutie isn't here yet, little brother."

"Figures. I could really use seeing Alex right now." Dal shrugged. "I'll live."

"You will. Oh, while we still have a few minutes, you want me to give you my report on your boy?"

"After Chase's little temper about that word, you're still gonna use it? And Alex isn't my 'boy.'"

Rhys shrugged, unrepentant.

Dal smirked but then sobered. "Now?"

Rhys nodded and pulled him back outside and around the edge of the building. "It's not good. Well, Alex's family is not good. He seems to be exactly what you said he is. He went to college, has a degree in culinary arts, and works for Dalton Harrison III as a personal chef. Alex is here every Saturday helping out. Rain, shine, it doesn't matter. From what I can find, unless he is seriously ill, he works. The only person constant in his life is a friend, Kai Holmes, and his boss."

"Okay, so Alex doesn't have a big circle of friends. I knew that already. What about the scars?"

Rhys didn't want to tell his little brother about the damn scars on his boyfriend's neck. "That's where the not good part comes in. In high school, Alex was a straight-A student, kind of a loner, but never in trouble of any kind. Then one day he turns up in Milwaukee, beat the hell up. I won't give you the gory details, but he ended up actually living at a teen shelter for a while."

Dal stood stock-still, barely breathing. "And the scars? Were they from his parents?"

"The records I could find say he refused to give up his attacker, but his parents didn't want to let him come home, so...."

"Oh God," Dal groaned. "I know. I see it all the time as a cop, but to think Alex went through something like that."

"He's got a twin sister, Lyric, but she married right out of high school and lives on the same street as his parents. Don't know her stance on what happened, though. I didn't do any interviewing that would let them know I was digging." Rhys checked his watch before looking around again. "One other thing, though. This has to do with Alex himself," he paused again, looking uncertain for once.

"Spit it out, Rhys. If something's wrong, I need to know."

"He often dresses as a woman at work and sometimes here at the center."

Dal burst out laughing, even though he didn't look happy. "I know that! And he's damn sexy either way."

"Huh, didn't think you went for queens or cross-dressing."

"Don't normally, but if you had seen Alex last night.... Actually, I'm glad you didn't because having you there would have been...." Dal shivered, and Rhys chuckled. "Actually, I wish I could put my finger on it, but it wasn't just the outfit. He seemed so different, yet the same. And this morning when he got up, he was all boy again."

"When he got up?" Rhys asked, waggling his brows at Dal. "Thought you were taking it 'slow' with Mr. Shy-and-Sexy?" Rhys made finger quotes in the air as he dragged the word out.

"We were, are, oh, never mind. My love life is none of your concern."

"You're my brother. Everything in your life is my business."

"Shouldn't we be getting ready?"

"Probably, but are you okay with what I told you?"

Dal sighed, then nodded. "I will be. I have to be for Alex's sake, but if they ever try anything again, I might need you to get me a good lawyer."

"That's not funny, Dal. You promised to behave if I did this for you. Now, come on, we have people to bounce and terrorize," he added, grinning, before he went back inside.

"DAL," RHYS said into the phone, hating the need to call him. It had only been a couple of days since the dance, but phoning anyone from the ER was never a good thing. Calling about your partner *and* your father was worse.

"What's up?"

"I'm at the ER with Chase and ran into Mom." The need to call his brother was confusing, as he didn't actually know what was wrong. "Dad's here, but she won't tell me why. I thought a combined force might get us more information, like why and where."

"Why is Chase in the ER? Wait, did you say Dad was in the hospital? What the hell for? Other than insane, he seemed fine when we saw him."

"I don't know what for," he ground out. "She won't tell me. Something about a promise to him not to."

"And Chase?"

"Oh, he fell on his bruised wrist. Seems it was a little worse than he led us to believe. Needless to say, I have to remind myself that going and killing the fucker isn't in Chase's best interest."

"I'll be there as soon as I can. I'm at Lexie's, so it won't take long," Dal replied and hung up.

"He'll be here soon, Chase, but I still wish you'd report this and press charges."

"Don't, okay? You're supposed to be babying me and stuff, not harassing me." Chase pouted, but Rhys could tell this time it was real. He felt like an ass for fighting with Chase. He was right. He should be trying to comfort him.

"All right, sweetheart. What can I do while we wait for the doctors to come back? Maybe you can get them to make your cast some cool color. I mean, I've seen everything from camo to dinos to stars and stripes. It won't be too bad, really."

"My job is based around my ability to type, Rhys. How the hell am I supposed to finish my current projects or work to keep the influx of business? One-handed isn't going to work!"

"Hey, now, no yelling. You're going to scare someone." Rhys thought about the issue, hoping his next words would be taken the way they were meant. "What about if I get you some of that software where you tell the computer what to do instead of typing it all? And, uh, maybe you could ask Grayson about working for you. He'd like that."

"Grayson is your friend and came here to help with the serial-killer case, not to babysit my consulting company. How long can he stay, anyway?"

The question gave Rhys hope that maybe Chase would listen. Besides, he'd love to have Grayson closer. "He took a leave of absence to come help out, but I'm sure you could talk him into staying longer. He hates it in DC. He only stays because it's where he'd been living."

Chase stared off into nothing for a few minutes, but Rhys refrained from pushing, knowing how Chase's mind worked at times like this. After a bit, he was rewarded for his patience. "I will talk to him. Really, I need another person or forty-hour days. And he's good enough. But I don't need your program. I have one I wrote myself that works for programming, which most wouldn't be any good for, but I won't be even half as fast as normal using it."

"That's fine. Talk to Grayson, hire a temp, whatever you need to do. Just don't mess up your wrist or hurt yourself trying to be Super Chase. Please."

"I'll be good, or try to be." Chase looked around the room and scowled. "Where's the damn doctor? I want to go home."

"I know, sweetheart. I know."

"Chase? Rhys? You two okay?" Dal said as he stormed through the door.

Chase looked up and frowned. "Yeah, your brother is just overly paranoid."

"You fell on the same arm that ass hat hurt, and it was bad enough you screamed and wouldn't let me touch it, even to see how severely it was damaged. Get over it, Chase," Rhys snapped.

"Rhys, chill." Dal turned to face Chase again. "What exactly is wrong with your wrist?"

"I just got back from X-ray," Chase sulked. "Seems it was already damaged, and when I fell, it created a hairline crack. We're waiting on someone to put it in a cast. Dammit!"

"Do you want to press charges? I mean, breaking your wrist is a lot more severe than a simple bruise."

"I don't—"

"Yes, you will. You would demand James did if it was him hurt. Do you think I care about your safety any less than you do about James's?"

"Of course I would," Chase snapped. "But his ex had a thing for hunting him down to hurt and terrorize him. I'll never see Jonathan, though."

"Chase," Dal interrupted again. "I won't make you report it, but if he broke your wrist over you coming to warn him he might be in danger, what might he be doing to his wife and kids when they act up?"

He snorted but looked up at Dal, his eyes cloudy, lips tight. "You really think it could be more than just him panicking I might out him?"

Dal shrugged. "Dunno, but he broke your wrist. That doesn't sound like someone I'd want near kids unchecked."

"I'll think about it. Right now, I just want to get through this," Chase said as a nurse and a doctor entered the small room. "Why don't you two go get some coffee, and Rhys can tell you about his parents while this nice man wraps my hand and arm in gross stuff."

"Yeah," Dal said. "That sounds good. Alex is waiting for me anyway."

Rhys grumbled, leaned down to kiss Chase's forehead, and followed Dal out.

HALF AN hour or so later, Chase was finally released from the hell the ER doctor put him through over a simple cast; though to be fair, the fact he asked for a rainbow cast was probably half the reason for the guy's attitude. Make a doctor raid the kiddie area? Yeah, he did, but looking down at his arm, he smiled, loving that if he had to wear the damn thing, at least it was colorful.

He was pulled out of his musings by Dal's deep voice. "Cute. Don't they have braces and things they could use instead of the big cast?"

"Probably, but the doctor insisted this was better and would limit my movements. He"—Chase rolled his eyes and nodded at Rhys—"convinced the doc I needed the big one. At least he was willing to take the time to make it pretty."

"It's cool," the beautiful light-skinned black man with Dal said softly. Chase looked him over quickly, pleased with what he saw, hoping this was Dal's new boyfriend. He was about Chase's height, thin but wiry. He also had soft brown eyes so light they were gold. Looks aside, it was the way he watched Dal that made Chase happy. Dal needed someone to love that would love him back, and this guy... yeah, he fit the bill nicely.

"Thanks. You're Alex, right? If we wait for these two to introduce us, we'll still be here next spring."

"Brat," Rhys grumbled, tousling his hair playfully.

Dal chuckled, "My apologies, guys. Chase, this is Alex Nobel. Lexie, this colorful character is Chase Manning, IT god, and he's crazy enough to be dating Rhys."

"So nice to meet you, Alex."

Alex nodded, a shy smile pulling at his lips. "Thanks."

"Damn, Dal, he's even cuter than Nikki," Chase said and grinned.

"Chase!" both Dal and Rhys groaned in unison. "Be good, please," Dal continued.

"What? He is. Cuter than her hubby or his brother too."

"I didn't date her husband," Dal defended.

"No, but you did date her and her brother-in-law," Chase countered. Teasing Dal was so much fun.

"She was an experiment or you're bi?" Alex asked, his voice soft, not meeting Dal's gaze.

"Bi, yeah. I dated Nikki a couple of years ago. She's Rhys's office person for his PI business. Is that a problem?" He shifted from foot to foot, and Chase instantly regretted his words.

"N-no, I just didn't know you liked girls too. Is that why—" He cut himself off, glancing over to where Chase and Rhys watched them.

"Why what?"

"Nothing. Don't you need to find your dad? I can go home if you like. One of them can probably drop you off to get your bike, if you'd rather."

Dal hesitated but then answered, "You don't have to stay, baby. I know you have your sister coming over tomorrow. Well, this morning. It's okay if you want to meet Mom another time."

Chase patted Dal on the arm. "Hey, big guy, why don't I take Alex for a quick bite and you two go do the parent thing. Your mom was acting really weird, and I don't think either of us," he added, gesturing to Alex and himself, "are going to help her feel better about talking right now."

Alex tensed and looked up at Dal, the question clear in his beautiful amber eyes.

Dal nodded. "Be careful, and Chase, be nice. Lexie means a lot to me."

"I know he does, Dal. You two go figure out what's up with your mom and dad, while we go grab some breakfast."

They all agreed, and Dal and Rhys walked Alex and Chase out. Once at the car, each man opened the door and gave a kiss to his respective partner. They took Alex's car, seeing as he'd driven Dal over and Chase wasn't ready to drive quite yet.

"Cancer?"

His mom nodded, tears still streaming down her cheeks. They sat in the family waiting area, not wanting to disturb their dad. Nor did they want her hiding behind their dad and not telling them what was going on. "We found out just before we left to visit family in Wales."

"Wait," Rhys growled. "You've known for months he has cancer and haven't said word one to either of us? He's *our* dad!"

"And he's my husband," she snapped. "He didn't want you to know yet. It's nonsense, but he wanted to wait until he didn't have a choice. Your dad hopes the treatments he is to start shortly will cure him."

"So he wouldn't have to ever say anything? Typical." Dal fumed, as did Rhys, but they both knew that was the way Bryn was. Never wanted to appear weak, not even when diagnosed with breast cancer—how did a man get that anyway? "Wait, Mom, is this what's behind his sudden push for me to marry and have kids?" Dal asked, paling dangerously in Rhys's opinion.

She blushed, looking down at her hand, which clutched wet tissues. She nodded.

"We'll do everything we can for Dad, but you can't let him bully Dal like this. It's not fair."

"I know," she sniffled. "I told him that, but he's determined to have grandkids before he... before he...." She burst into tears again, shaking with her sobs.

Dal wrapped her in his arms, rocking her gently as they both tried to comfort her. An eternity later, she finally calmed but clutched them both to her. "I can't lose him," she stated, her voice ruined from all the tears.

"There's so much that can be done, Mom. We will get him the best doctors in the world. I promise," Dal murmured, Rhys rumbling his agreement.

They gave her a few minutes to freshen up. When she rejoined them, she sat next to Dal and took his hand, patting it. "Sweetheart, can't you just go along with things for your dad's sake? Once he's better, you can break it off with the girl if you really want."

He pulled away, worrying his cuticle as he spoke. "I—" He snapped his mouth shut and looked around the room, desperation in his eyes.

"He'll think about it, okay?" Rhys interjected. He wasn't about to let his father's illness destroy his brother and his chance at happiness.

"We just want you happy, baby, and you would make a great father."

"Thanks," Dal mumbled, not looking up.

"And it would mean so much to your dad," she continued, seemingly having no clue how her words were wounding his baby brother. "But, if you stick around, your father will realize you know about his health. Let me be the one to tell him, not have him wake to the two of you stalking his room."

"We'll go for now," Rhys commented, his hand a firm pressure on Dal's shoulder. "But we won't keep this hidden for long. He should have his family around him, supporting him. And Dal will consider dating to keep him calm. Deal?"

"Agreed, Rhys. Dal?" She looked at Dal, hope clear in her eyes.

Dal took a deep breath and then nodded. "I'll see what I can do to make things easier for him. That's the best I can promise right now."

She beamed at him, hugged them both, and wished them a good rest of their night. She waved to them as they left her outside their father's hospital room door.

chapter twenty-one

"SIMON," CHASE grumbled.

"Don't you dare 'Simon' me. We've barely seen you lately, and you've kept that sexy beast of yours practically hidden. I know I wasn't up for dealing with him the last time I was over, when he came to get you, but you're our friend." Simon put his hands on his hips as he continued fussing. "And if he's this damn important to you suddenly, then we need to get to know him better."

Chase knew Si was right, he just hated that his friends knew only the bad stuff about Rhys, not how sweet or protective or loyal the man was. They didn't need to know how delicious or ravenous, though, and he knew that was the kind of gossip Si most loved. "I already have to take him to meet Mom, I suppose I can arrange something for you and the guys too. I mean, you've already met him."

"Yeah, when he hurt you." Si rolled his eyes and sighed. "Now that things are working out so you two are a couple, it's different."

"All right. How about dinner and drinks? Eat, visit, get to know each other…. But no being mean to him, Si." When Simon grinned, Chase added, "I mean it, Simon. I won't have you picking on him, making him feel like an outsider. I—" He stumbled to a halt as what he'd almost said reverberated through his mind and heart.

"You what, babe?"

"I-I think I love him," Chase whispered. His knees threatened to give out on him as he grabbed the kitchen counter in Simon's apartment.

"Oh, dear," Simon murmured, grabbing a stool and guiding Chase onto it. "Like love with the dick or love with the heart?"

"I don't play at relationships, and you know it, Si," Chase snapped, irritated that his friend was on one of his 'love isn't real' kicks lately. He understood, really. Being dumped like he had had to hurt, but Rhys wasn't like that.

"I know," Si soothed. "I didn't mean it that way, no matter what I sounded like. I'm just surprised is all. You haven't told him yet, have you?"

Chase shook his head. "Not really. He knows I care about him and I trust him, but no, I haven't said the words."

"Do you think he feels the same?"

He thought about that for a minute, concluding that yes, Rhys had to love him. "I think so. You haven't seen how he is around me or how he's been with all the murder insanity. I mean, he picked me up, carried me to the car, and even buckled me in when I fell and made this thing worse," Chase explained, brandishing his brightly colored cast. "He tried to kill that ass of a cop the other day. And how he is when we do nothing...."

"Yeah, even with everything bad lately, you've smiled more since you two finally started seeing each other than you have in years. So, what ya going ta do about it?" Simon asked, right brow arched so high Chase wanted to smack him.

"Keep working on us, I guess. I mean, we're practically living together as it is. Well, until all this serial stuff is done."

"Do you want to move back to your nice but empty apartment or stay in that big loft of his you told me about?"

"I don't know."

"Yes, you do. Don't BS me. Where do you want to be?"

"It doesn't matter. We aren't to that point yet, and I've never lived with a boyfriend. Stayed over, sure, but not lived with."

Simon draped his arm about Chase's shoulder. "You tell me not to worry how fast the guys in the stories I write fall in love or move to the happily ever after stage, that love has its own timetable. Why would you think your heart had one? Or that his does, for that matter? If he is the one for you, then don't let my moping influence you. Make him your partner instead of just your boyfriend."

Chase thought for a minute and then smiled. He looked at his friend, wishing Si could feel the happiness Rhys gave him. "Thanks, hun."

"I didn't do anything. Now, go home and get your man."

He hugged Simon tight, hoping Si could find the same happiness he had with Rhys. "I think I'll stop and get lunch and then go back to Rhys's. I think it's time we had a talk." Chase laughed when he thought about how Rhys would hate being told that.

On his way over, he decided to stop and eat at Jake's Deli. He hadn't been there in a while, and with all the weirdness lately, he wanted something familiar. He sent Rhys a text, letting him know he would be back in a bit and asking if he wanted to come over to his place. He'd barely been home in days, and he was tired of the limited supply of clothes and body products he had at Rhys's.

He got through the line quickly and sat at one of the small tables, intending to dig into his tuna on wheat-berry when a shadow fell over his food. He was startled to see Jonathan again.

"Mind if I sit?" The tone didn't match the scowl on Jonathan's face, but he figured since they were in public, he was relatively safe. He nodded.

"Here," Jonathan said, reaching for his empty cup. "I'll get your drink, then we can talk."

"All right," he agreed, confused at the man's actions, but then Jonathan had stopped making sense to him when they were still teens. He didn't figure he had any chance of figuring him out now.

HE WAS cold, and God, did his head hurt! *What the hell?* Chase tried to roll over but found he couldn't move. Fighting down the terror threatening, he cracked open his eyes to find it was pitch-dark, wherever he was.

Chase took a moment to assess his body and his lack of mobility, realizing his hands and feet were bound, but with no lights, he wasn't certain with what. He was gagged, and that, more than the dark or the binding, had him freaking out in seconds. He couldn't seem to get enough air, no matter how hard he tried, nor could he calm down.

Moments later, the world faded until he heard only his own panicked breathing. Then he heard nothing.

CHASE CAME to again, a sharp undulating pain blossoming through his side over and over. He struggled to get out of the way of whatever was attacking him, but he was still unable to move. He cried out, begging around the gag in his mouth for whoever was there to stop please.

"Sick, filth!" a voice screamed above him. "Have to exorcise you! Remove your stain from my life so I can be clean again," the voice continued.

Unable to move away from the blows, Chase screamed as the pain increased in his side, ribs, and head, until the world went blank, and even the pain could no longer reach him.

WHEN CHASE fought his way back to consciousness, he regretted having done so immediately. He was still on his side, bound as before, but the gag was rancid. It was painfully obvious to him he'd lost at least part of his lunch during the attack earlier, and he was thankful he hadn't had much before this insanity began. Sadly, he was still in complete darkness, so he had no clue how long he'd been there. Hours, days—time had no meaning right then.

He tried to shift so his casted wrist wasn't pinned under him, but the only movement he managed caused the pain to spike sharply and the world to spin until inner darkness swallowed him again.

RHYS PACED inside Chase's apartment, cell clutched in his fist, and tried not to panic. When he'd arrived that evening, he had expected Chase to be there. Chase's bike was there, but his car was missing, and he hadn't answered the door. He also hadn't answered his phone any of the dozen times Rhys had called. And while he'd been able to convince the super to let him into Chase's apartment, there was no sign he had been there in days.

He froze at the loud ringing. He almost dropped the phone in his haste to answer the call. "Chase?"

"No, Rhys. I did find his car, though," Mark said.

"What? Where?" Where the hell was he!

"At one of the little delis he likes to hit for lunch, but that's the only thing that's normal here. The manager said he argued with some big guy, and they left together before Chase finished his food."

"Big guy? So he left with a friend?" Please be a friend. "Something wrong with his car?"

"The manager said the guy with Chase practically had to carry him out."

"But Chase was...."

"Rhys," Mark countered. "I've never known you to be blind to reality, man."

He nodded as fear gripped him, sealing his breath. "We need to call his friends."

Twenty minutes later, Mark, Grayson, and Dal stood in Chase's living room.

"What do we know, Rhys?" Dal asked.

"Not much, unfortunately. They refused to let Mark see the security footage, and no one will let me go over there."

"That's because you getting arrested for attempted murder won't help find Chase, Rhys," Grayson countered.

"Whatever. We need to see if they got who this guy was on the tape or maybe even footage from the parking area. I want Chase back, now!"

"Focus, Rhys," Mark interrupted Rhys's fit. "Dal can try to find a way to get us those tapes. Right, Dal?"

Dal stopped pacing and looked at Mark. "He's an adult, Mark. Until he's been officially missing for twenty-four hours...."

"Fuck that," Rhys roared. "You know something's wrong! We can't wait that long. He could be—" He broke off, unable to allow his thoughts to go there. "It has to be now!"

"I know he...." Dal faced Rhys and sighed, rubbing his hands over his face. "You're right. Of course. I'll see what I can do, but when I get fired for this, you're going to have a new business partner," he grumbled.

Rhys knew Dal hated going against protocol, but Chase's life was worth more to him than his brother's damn job. He knew Dal would expect the same from him. "Good. Now, did anyone get hold of his mom...?"

The three men discussed strategy while Dal took off to see what he could manage to get from the deli. Less than an hour later, they knew who had Chase and a rough idea of where Chase most likely was, thanks to Grayson's computer skills. Rhys made a mental note never to tease the man for his geek tendencies again.

CHASE STARTLED awake when he heard shouting. The noise was far away and no one was kicking or hitting him. It took a little while to clear his head enough to make out the sounds, but when he did, they made no sense to him. It seemed as if someone had the TV turned way up and a cop show was on. There was screaming about putting hands up and weapons down. There was also shouting about having to find someone, but he couldn't focus enough to keep up with all the yelling.

He hurt so bad he shook, and his head felt as if it were two sizes too small for his skull. After a few more moments, he realized it wasn't a show, it was people outside the area he was trapped in. In desperation, he started screaming around the gag still in his mouth. His voice was muffled, but he still gave it his all, hoping it would be enough to bring someone to him.

He froze midyell when he heard loud popping sounds nearby. He assumed it was a gun. The thought made him silent, though. What if it wasn't someone come to rescue him? What if the crazy person he was being held by shot whoever had just broken in and then shot him?

Shaking so hard he could barely drag in air, Chase decided to stay quiet, hoping whoever was outside were the good guys or the cops and not worse than his current warden.

The silence after the second set of shots was deafening and only served to make him panic worse. When he heard someone screaming again, he was confused. It sounded like Rhys yelling at Dal. That couldn't be right. Why would Rhys be mad at Dal, and how would either of them know where to find him? He didn't even know where he was.

Chase guessed he must have passed out again, because when he came to, the lights were on and painfully bright after all the darkness.

There were people all around him, talking and shouting. "Hold him still so I can get this crap off him," a gruff voice ordered. It took a moment before he realized it was Mark speaking.

"I'm trying! He won't hold still, and he's a lot stronger than he looks." That was Grayson.

"Chase, man, hold still," Mark said. "I don't want to hurt you worse than you already are. Okay?"

He calmed, hoping this was real and not that his mind had snapped. Someone moved him onto his back carefully. It hurt like hell, but at least no one hit him again.

"Here," a different voice said, and the gag was removed. The sudden object over his face that followed had him flailing. He didn't want anything binding him again.

"Chase," Mark yelled. "It's just oxygen. The paramedic is a nice guy and is trying to help you. Understand?"

Paramedic? Help? Those at least made sense. He stilled again, desperate to hold on long enough to find Rhys. They moved him onto a board and then onto something that rolled, one of those gurneys, he assumed.

"Rhys?" he finally managed to ask, sounding slurred enough he worried they might not understand him. He tried again anyway. "Where's Rhys?"

"Don't worry, he's here. He's with Dal in the other room."

It didn't make sense. Why wouldn't he be here with him instead of Mark and Grayson? "Is he hurt?" he gasped out, shaking hard again. *No, please no! Rhys has to be okay! I didn't get to tell him I love him yet. He can't be hurt!*

"Breathe, Chase. Rhys is fine. He's fine. Not a mark on him, I swear," Mark said, strained and rushed.

Chase tried to focus, but breathing hurt, and being moved only made it worse. "Please. I need. See. Rhys," he panted, struggling to stay awake and focused.

"I'll try to get him," Grayson said before disappearing from Chase's narrow view. Mark stayed next to him even as the paramedics rolled him out into the night air and to the waiting ambulance.

He was confused when Mark disappeared but then elated when Rhys appeared beside him, until he noticed the red stuff all over Rhys's hands. "You're hurt!"

"Chase, sweetheart. Don't try to talk. Just rest now." Rhys's face was tearstained as he stared down at Chase.

"Blood," Chase managed to force out.

"I'm fine. It's not mine. Now rest, please." Rhys brushed his cheek, but with such a featherlight touch, Chase could barely feel it. He let out a sigh and closed his eyes, certain Rhys would protect him.

He felt the banging when they closed the doors and the vehicle started to move, but he lost his tentative hold on the waking world. His last thought was that Rhys's touch was the best thing he'd ever felt, and he would do anything to keep him.

chapter twenty-two

"HOW COULD you not tell me what was going on until afterward?" James yelled, his voice high and angry in a way Chase had never heard before.

"I didn't want you to worry," Rhys rumbled. "Seriously, you just got married and all. He wouldn't want to take away from your happy."

"Great, so my best friend ends up kidnapped and hurt, but what everyone's worried about is me? Am I the only one who thinks that's nuts?"

Chase listened to the two most important men in his life argue, unable to get his mouth to work.

"It's not like I knew this would happen. I wouldn't have let him out of my sight otherwise! I have never been so afraid."

"I know, Rhys." James's voice dropped to the soothing, "it will all be okay" tone Chase knew well. "I'm sorry for yelling at you. This isn't your fault, it's his crazy ex's."

Chase was finally able to make his mouth work, though it felt like the Sahara had moved in while he was out. "Rhys? James?" God! Could he sound any worse?

Twin gasps from across the room sounded before both men were at his side. When he forced his eyes to focus, he took in James's pained face and Rhys's ashen one. Both looked like nervous wrecks.

"Water?"

"Right here," Rhys said, holding a straw to his lips. When his throat felt a little more usable, he murmured, "I'm sorry."

Rhys took his free hand, rubbing his thumb over the back of it. "Cariadon?"

He smiled at Rhys, loving that he was precious enough to Rhys for such a special pet name. "Don't fight." He shifted his head enough to meet James's eyes and added, "Please."

"Sorry, sweetheart," Rhys said at the same time James said, "Sorry, Chase."

"What happened?" The two men shared a look that screamed worry as far as Chase could tell. "Tell me."

"What do you remember?" Rhys asked as James moved around him to sit in the chair pulled close to the bed.

Chase searched his memories, fuzzy things that they were. "I hung out with Si, then left to go to your place. I had something to talk to you about." He paused, hoping his head would stop hurting so much. "But, uh, I stopped to eat and ran into Jonathan. Uh...." He couldn't come up with how he'd ended up in that horrible place or who would want to hurt him like that. "Then being somewhere dark and someone kicking me. Then nothing until you all showed up to get me." A flash of Rhys in the ambulance made him flinch. "Wait, you had blood on you. Who's blood, Rhys?"

"Jonathan took you to a warehouse he owns and had you bound in one of the back rooms."

"He's the one who...." *Why would he do that?* "He wanted to protect his secrets so badly, why risk something so insane?"

"He's on a different floor from you. I've not been allowed near him again to find out the why of it," Rhys growled. "I failed to protect you," he added, looking down and away from Chase.

"This isn't your fault, Rhys," James said softly. "Until we know why he did this, we have no way to know what triggered this attack."

"When he broke Chase's wrist, I should have known the man wouldn't quit so easily."

"Hindsight is always twenty-twenty," James countered. "You can't play these what-if and shoulda-woulda-coulda games."

"Listen to James, please. This isn't anyone's fault but the person who did this." Chase thought through what they'd said so far and realized neither man had explained the blood yet. He clutched Rhys's hand tighter. "And the blood?"

"That ass opened fire on Dal and hit his shoulder. We're waiting to hear how bad the damage is, but he'll be fine," Rhys said, still not meeting his eyes.

"Oh God! Dal?"

"Hey, hey, Chase," James said, shaking him gently. "Calm down. He's out of surgery, and the doctor is in with Rhys and Dal's parents. We are waiting to hear more."

"You're sure?"

"He is," said a new voice from the doorway. There was a stocky, older black man standing there. Chase recognized him right away as Dal's boss. "Hello, son," he said, nodding to Rhys.

"Sir? Do you know any more?" Rhys asked.

"Yes and no. I don't know what the doctors say about Dal's shoulder yet, but I'm rather impressed with his aim if he really did shoot that ass upstairs after he was shot," the captain said, heavy brows raised in question.

"Ballistics will verify whose gun did what, so there's no reason for the questions."

"True, but I'm still surprised he went along with your little rescue plan instead of calling it in. Once you had the tape, it was no longer a question of willful disappearance."

"Couldn't afford to take the time, sir. Is he in trouble?"

Chase watched and listened, but the idea Dal would be punished for helping rescue him was beyond his ability to keep quiet. "You can't go after Dal for doing what's right!"

The captain looked from Rhys to Chase, a small sad smile on his face. "Son, it's not up to me what does or doesn't happen. It's a matter for IA and the lawyers to work out. He was off duty and chose his path on this one. He knew what he risked by doing things Rhys's way instead of by the book. But," he said, holding his hand up to hush Chase's protests. "I will fight tooth and nail to protect him."

There was a long pause as everyone digested the facts presented. Finally, Chase looked up and asked the question he most wanted to know since he'd woken up in the dark. "Why'd he do that to me?"

"It wasn't just you he hurt," the older man explained. "We found evidence that ties him to all but one of the killings your partner's been investigating."

"But why?"

"Something about purging the past so he can be clean. It's all he's said so far. We don't know anything else yet. I'm sorry. The only other thing I can tell you is you're safe now. There were no signs he was working with anyone, so you have no need to fear him any longer."

Chase didn't understand what that meant any more than the screaming before had made any sense to him. What he did know was he would be eternally thankful to Rhys and Dal for getting him out of that horrible place.

After that, things were hectic for a while as nurses and doctors came in and poked, prodded, and fussed both at and over him. He dozed off and on as well. The next time he came fully awake, instead of James in the chair, his mom was there. While happy to see her, he was a bit confused and hurt that Rhys and James weren't still with him.

"Morning, sweetie," his mom said, her smoky voice strained as if she'd been crying.

"Mom?"

"That nice young man of yours is just outside, arguing with his folks about not leaving you, and James is in with Dal right now. No one will let either of you be alone," she added, her lips curving in a slight smile.

"You met Rhys?"

"Yes, and he's simply lovely. Or, I guess handsome would be better, considering how rugged he seems."

He sighed, thankful she liked Rhys, especially given the circumstances. "I'm glad. This wasn't how I wanted you two to meet."

"Didn't think it was. Now, I wanted to let you know why your dad isn't here. He is trying to get back, but planes being what they are, he has been delayed a little. He will be here as soon as he can, though, so don't think ill of him."

"Mom! I have never thought badly of Dad. Well, no more than any normal kid does some days. He's the best, just like you were the most wonderful mom ever."

Her smile was real and full this time, tears leaking down her cheeks. "This is twice now I've thought we were going to lose you. You have to be more careful, sweetheart. My poor heart can't take all this. Neither can your body," she added pointedly.

Yeah, he was a mess, though luckily it was mostly just severe bruising, not all broken and punctured like he'd feared. Still, they'd told him he had a concussion, and he'd be sore for ages and look wonderful at the same time. "I know. But this wasn't my fault."

"I know it wasn't. Your boyfriend said you had been helping with the investigation until recently."

"He's more than that to me, Mom."

"In what way?"

"In the 'I'm going to ask him to move in with me' way, or if I can move in with him since he has a house, I guess."

She gasped, but a much deeper one from across the room drowned out the sound. Rhys and his father were standing there. Rhys's mouth hung open, but Bryn's face was downright gleeful.

"H-hi, Rhys."

"Really, cariadon?"

"Yeah," he sighed, nervous but determined. "That's what I'd wanted to talk to you about that night. Last night, I guess, or was it the one before." He still didn't know what day it was. "Anyway, I wanted to talk to you about making our living together a permanent thing."

"I'd lo—like that. You'll need the help for a bit anyway."

Chase frowned, not liking the implication Rhys would have him stay out of duty or some such nonsense. "That's not why, Rhys."

Rhys moved over to his side and carefully wrapped him in his arms. "I didn't mean it that way, sweetheart. I would love for you to live with me. I can get movers to get your things before I bring you home," he continued. He looked over at Bryn and asked, "Dad? You have people you trust I could hire, right?"

"I'll make some calls if that's all right with your partner."

Chase's head spun at how fast things were suddenly moving. "We can worry about it once I'm out and better, hun."

Rhys shook his head before Chase had finished speaking. "You'll want your stuff and clothes and all. Besides, you really think I'm going to let you try to help? Not happening. I'll ask James to supervise, okay? He'll know what's what in your old place, and then you can have the fun of helping me find places for your things once you're home."

He took in the naked hope in Rhys's eyes and smiled. "Okay. But only if James agrees."

"Thank you, Chase." Rhys hugged him tighter but was still careful with him.

"Come on, Mama Manning," Bryn murmured. "Let's leave these two to their planning. They don't need us for a few minutes."

"That's fine. I would like to check on that sweet boy of yours that got hurt saving my baby anyway. And it's Desiree, not Mama," she said, smiling. "I'll be back in a little, dear," she added, patting Chase carefully.

"Thanks, Mom."

Once they were alone again, he clutched Rhys's hand. "I had more I planned to say that night. And while this isn't the best place for heart-to-heart talks, it'll have to do."

"What else did you want to discuss? You said you wanted to live with me—was there more?"

"I'd come to the conclusion while talking to Simon that no matter how rocky a start we had, I needed to tell you how I felt and what I wanted. That I needed to stop letting my fears mess with our future."

"O... kay," Rhys said with a small nod. "So what other fears are a problem? I thought things were good between us."

"They are, Rhys. That's not what I meant. Si asked if I thought you loved me and if I loved you, and it was then I realized I wasn't falling for you, I was already in love with you." As soon as the words were out, he started to panic again. What if Rhys didn't feel the same? What if he wasn't ready to hear what Chase felt? What if all this had changed how Rhys felt....

"Cariadon, calm down. Take a deep breath." Chase focused on doing as ordered. Once his breathing was mostly normal, Rhys continued. "I love you too, ya twit. I only didn't say it before because I was afraid you'd run again." He leaned down and pressed his lips to Chase's in the sweetest kiss Chase had ever known. It was soft, closed mouthed, but still brought a joy to his bruised heart he hadn't known possible.

When they parted again, Rhys rested his forehead against Chase's. "I will tend to everything and have you moved in as soon as possible. Thank you."

"You've got to stop saying thanks for things like that, hun. This isn't a favor, it's our future. 'Kay?"

"Yes, Chase."

"Good boy."

Rhys growled softly. "Not a boy."

"Baby, you're my boy. That's not a bad thing, is it? Being mine?"

He shook his head. "I love you too."

LATER THAT night, he conned Rhys into taking him over to visit Dal. Getting permission wasn't the easiest thing, nor was moving to the wheelchair, thanks to how battered he was. But eventually he approached the door to Dal's room, Rhys right behind him.

Rhys stepped around him and knocked on the door before pushing it open and wheeling him in. His first look at Dal had Chase torn between laughing and crying. Dal was propped up in the hospital bed, but curled around him was Alex, his new boyfriend. They were absolutely adorable.

Before he could tell Rhys to take him back to his room, Dal's gaze met his. "Hey, Chase," he murmured. "Come in, but try to not wake Lexie, please. He passed out a little while ago."

"He's so sweet like that," Rhys said, stepping around so he could sit beside Chase. "How ya doing, little brother?"

"Not too bad, considering. And well, something good came from all this mess, other than Chase being home safe. Dad met Alex and promised to drop his campaign to have me married off and making little baby Sayers."

"Good. Still can't believe he tried to do that to you. Anyway, Chase has been bugging me, the nurses, his mom, and anyone else he could corner into letting him visit."

"Thanks for the intro, big guy." Chase chuckled, then stopped short, reminded painfully that his ribs were severely bruised.

"Careful," both men warned.

"It's okay. I just wanted to check on you and say how sorry I am you got hurt. Are you in a lot of trouble?"

"They're not sure the shoulder will heal up enough to let me go back to work as a beat cop, but," Dal paused, eying Alex a moment. "I wouldn't have been staying much longer anyway, so I'll be okay."

"You love being a cop, Dal. Don't play games with me, mister."

"I do love it, but it's not what I want to do forever anymore. I got my prelaw degree not that long ago. I spoke to Dad and Mel about it, and I'm not going back to work here. I don't think Alex will be too upset about my career change, once I tell him."

"He doesn't know?" Rhys asked, beating Chase to the punch.

"No, and I don't want either of you telling him either," he added with a frown. "I want to surprise him once I get my letter."

"Means I have to wait to throw you a party too, huh?"

"Yeah, Chase, it does. But I promise to let you know as soon as I know, all right?"

Chase nodded. "I really am sorry you got hurt."

"I know, as am I. It's not as if I went in there thinking 'oh, hey, can I get shot today,' though. We just wanted you safe and home."

"Thank you," he barely got out, choking back tears.

Rhys stood quickly, wrapping Chase in his strong arms. "Calm down, sweetheart. He gave us all a good fright, but he'll be fine."

Chase nodded against Rhys's chest, thankful to be alive and in Rhys's arms again. "I know. I was so scared I would never get to tell you I love you or see you again. Sorry for being such a little girl."

epilogue

Six months later

CHASE PACED as he waited for Rhys to get home so they could turn around and head right back out. It was their first Christmas together, and all three of their families demanded appearances. Tonight, they visited James and Seth and a few close friends; tomorrow, for brunch, they were at his parents; and then for dinner, they would go to Rhys's parents' house and meet up with not only his parents, but Dal and Alex, as well as Mark, Amber, and her parents.

He returned to their bedroom—still giddy at being able to call it *theirs*—to make sure Rhys's outfit was laid out and perfect. He knew Rhys would be happy in his leather and denim, but James's husband's friends and family expected a bit more formality than most. *At least it's a small gathering of close friends and family and not some huge corporate gala-style party*, he mused.

As he continued to ramble around their top-floor loft, he turned to memories of their life since that horrid night everything had changed for so many people he cared for and loved. The night he had been shot by Jonathan, Dal made a decision that ended his police career, but even with the pain, legal and physical, he'd suffered, Dal was happier now than he had ever been. He told Chase every time they spoke how thrilled he was to be with Alex in Chicago, attending law school.

Things at home had been, for the most part, blissful. He and Rhys had been living together since the moment he left the hospital. Grayson now worked for him full-time, though he still thought the man way too secretive.

What hadn't gone so well was the fallout of what Jonathan had done before "that night." He had killed three men, two of whom had been Chase's exes. It took a lot of time and psychiatric care and work to get out of Jonathan why he'd done what he had. What it came down to was the damage of his teen years with his family mixing with his mental instability and the insane abuse and "reprogramming" he'd suffered in one of those "cure the gay" programs.

Jonathan had never revealed why he had taken Chase but not killed him, as he had the others, but Chase was thankful every day. He made a point to tell Rhys he loved him regularly, now knowing how delicate life really was.

The front door clicked before Rhys entered their front room with a heavy tread. "Hey, cariadon," Rhys said as he dropped his leather coat on the couch. He brushed his lips against Chase's briefly and then hurried into their bedroom. Moments later, the shower turned on. Chase had to remind himself they didn't have time for him to join Rhys in the hot water right then.

A few minutes later, Rhys was out, dressed in the black dress slacks, emerald button-down silk shirt, and black-and-green tie Chase had bought him earlier that week. He had his dress coat over his arm and his polished boots in hand as he sauntered into the living room and sat to finish getting ready. When finished, he looked up and grinned. "Damn, sweetheart. You sure we have to go?" he asked as his gaze stripped Chase bare.

"Come on, big guy. We're going to be late if we don't leave now. I'll ravage you when we get home. For now, though," he continued, holding out Rhys's long cashmere overcoat.

"You know, they won't be upset if we aren't there twenty minutes early."

"We won't be early, but I refuse to be late. Now, get that sexy ass of yours moving," he added and slapped Rhys on said tush. Chase made sure to grab the bags of presents before they left the loft, took the steps out to Rhys's car, and then drove over to James's.

When they pulled up outside James's stone cottage, Chase took a moment to look at the lights through the window. He'd helped James hang them, though no one else had been allowed to place the doves, ribbons, glass ornaments, and more. Only James knew where each piece went, but Chase had had a blast watching his best friend work hard to make the perfect holiday wonderland in his home.

"Stop staring, would ya? It's freezing out here." Rhys didn't wait for him to move. He draped his arm over Chase's shoulder and led him to the ornately decorated door.

Moments later, it swung open to reveal Danni, James's stepdaughter, decked out in her red-and-gold dress, ribbons, and glittery red shoes. "Hi, Uncle Rhys. Hi, Uncle Chase."

"Hey, sweet pea," Rhys rumbled. He bent and scooped her up as they entered the great room.

"Oh, good. You made it." James maneuvered to Chase and embraced him tightly.

"When have I not been here for one of your holidays?" Chase asked, smirking.

"Um, never? Still, you could have decided to stay in tonight. Thanks for coming."

"No thanks required, Jamie. Now, let me put these down, and I'll be in to help you finish up."

James laughed and hugged him again. "It's all done, dear. Now, hurry up. We promised Danni everyone could have one present before dinner."

Twenty minutes later, they all had drinks—Danni's the only non-alcoholic one—and had gathered around the huge main tree. Chase expected Seth or James to hand out the gifts, but instead, Danni bounced over to Rhys, looking up at him through her long lashes.

"Is it time, Uncle Rhys?"

"Yes, baby." He hugged her before he handed her a small, chunky box he pulled from his inside coat pocket. "Deliver this for me like we practiced."

She nodded, a serious look on her pixie face. She skipped to where Chase sat, curtsied, and held out the gift. "You have to open this first," she whispered.

Chase looked around, confused, but followed her directions. When he'd gotten the wrapping out of the way and opened the small box, he was even more confused. Inside was one of those 3D red glass heart puzzles, already put together. "Um, thanks, sweetie."

Danni shook her head and smiled again. "You already have my heart," she paused to look at Rhys again before continuing. "Cariadon. This one is to remind you of what you have." Rhys reached over and handed her a second box, but it was Danni who spoke again. "This is to show everyone else." She held out the second box and giggled.

Chase looked at Rhys and asked, "Rhys, what's all this?"

"Just open it, and then I'll tell you."

Nervous, but a little excited as well, he slipped the ribbon off the box and opened it. What he found inside made his head spin and his pulse race. A matched set of platinum bands with tiny Welsh dragons engraved around them was nestled on a pillow of velvet. He stared at them, then back at Rhys, confused. They had talked about marriage, and Rhys had said until Wisconsin made it legal, he wasn't interested in getting married, so the rings made no sense to Chase.

"Breathe, sweetheart. This isn't a proposal, exactly. In my heart, you're already mine, just as I know I am yours. This is a promise. I promise to love you and only you for as long as I live. You are my heart. My center. My everything." Rhys paused and cleared his throat. His voice was rough when he spoke again. "Will you wear my promise to you?"

Unable to find his voice, Chase nodded, shoved his left hand out, and wiggled his fingers.

"I love you, cariadon," Rhys murmured as he slipped the band onto Chase's ring finger. "And I want the world to know it. Thank you."

Chase watched as the ring slid into place, overwhelmed by how his life had changed in so short a time. The ring matched the platinum wrist cuff he now wore—a gift from Rhys when he'd first moved in.

"Uncle Chase? You're supposed to put the big ring on Uncle Rhys now," Danni stage-whispered.

He let out a shaky breath and hugged her tightly. "Thank you, pixie." He took the other ring and slipped it into place on his lover's finger.

The room burst into applause and whoops of joy as Rhys leaned in and sealed his lips over Chase's, pressing and nibbling lightly. With a teasing flick to his lip ring, Rhys pulled back and rested his forehead against Chase's. His heart melted a little more, and for the first time in his life, he truly believed in miracles.

Coming Soon
by Tempeste O'Riley

Temptations of Desire

Desires Entwined: Book Three

Alexander James Noble is a gender fluid gay man who gave up on finding Mister Right a long time ago. He's not asking for much, though. He just wants a guy who loves all of him and appreciates his feminine form too.

At the local LGBTQ center where Alex regularly volunteers, he meets Dal Sayer, an officer of the Milwaukee PD. Because he's been rejected one too many times, Alex doesn't trust the huge cop and the interest he shows in him, but once Dal sets his mind on something, he goes all out. Pushing aside his preconceived notions, Alex opens up just a little and soon caves.

From their first date—while dealing with his father's failing health and his parents' demands for him to settle down and have children—Dal never takes his eyes off his goal of making Alex his. But proving to Alex he isn't like all the men who couldn't see him for who he truly was and only wanted to hide him away is harder than he thought.

TEMPESTE O'RILEY is an out and proud omnisexual/bi woman whose best friend growing up had the courage to do what she couldn't—defy the hate and come out. He has been her hero ever since.

Tempe is a hopeless romantic who loves strong relationships and happily-ever-afters. Though new to writing M/M, she has done many things in her life, yet writing has always drawn her back—no matter what else life has thrown her way. She counts her friends, family, and Muse as her greatest blessings in life. She lives in Wisconsin with her children, reading, writing, and enjoying life.

Tempe is also a proud member of Romance Writers of America® and Rainbow Romance Writers.

Learn more about Tempeste and her writing at http://tempesteoriley.com or on Facebook.

Don't Miss

TEMPESTE O'RILEY

DESIGNS
of
DESIRE

http://www.dreamspinnerpress.com

Don't Miss

TEMPESTE O'RILEY

BOUND
by
DESIRE

DESIRES ENTWINED SERIES

Romance from DREAMSPINNER PRESS

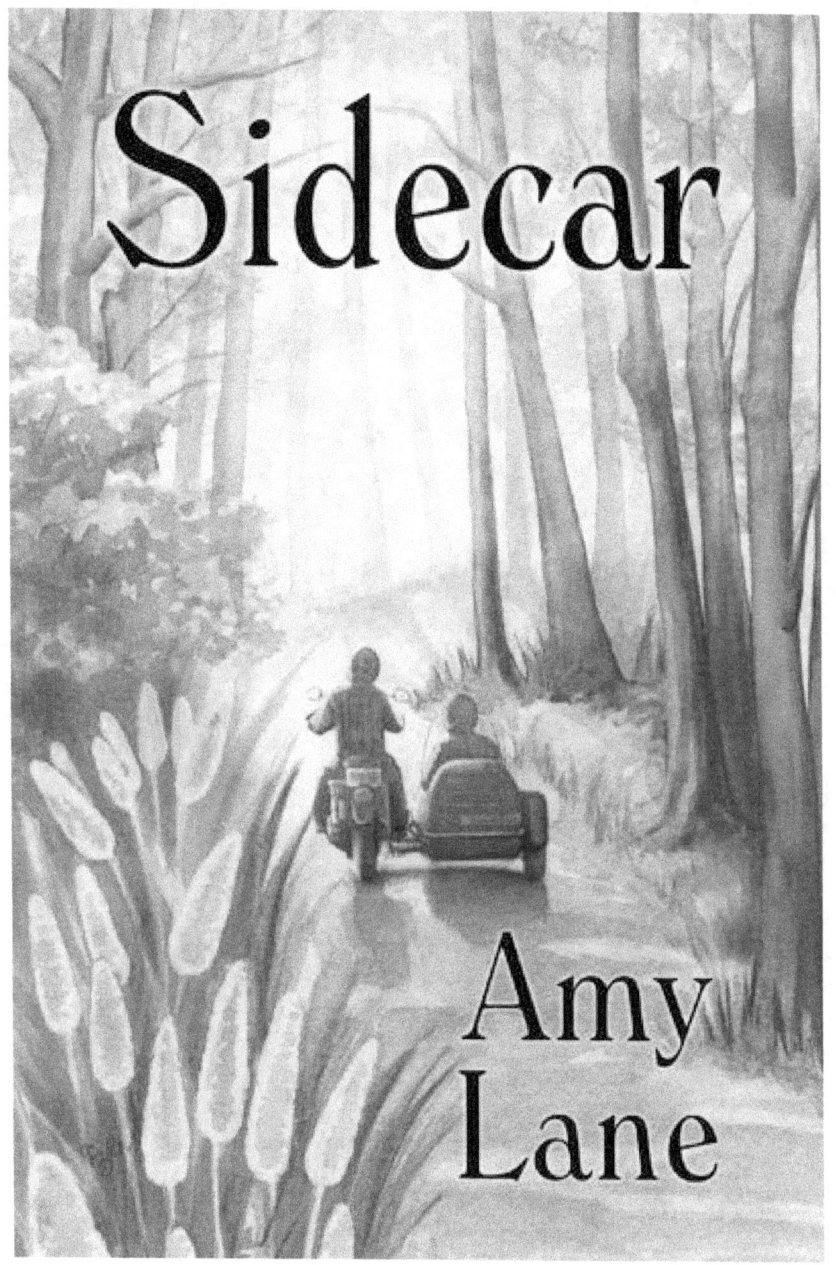

Sidecar

Amy Lane

http://www.dreamspinnerpress.com

www.ingramcontent.com/pod-product-compliance
Lightning Source LLC
Chambersburg PA
CBHW060058260626
47160CB00005B/1711